Vengeful Spirits

AND A

Lost Gold Mine

MJ MILLER

For Eric. 10 Down, 90 to go.

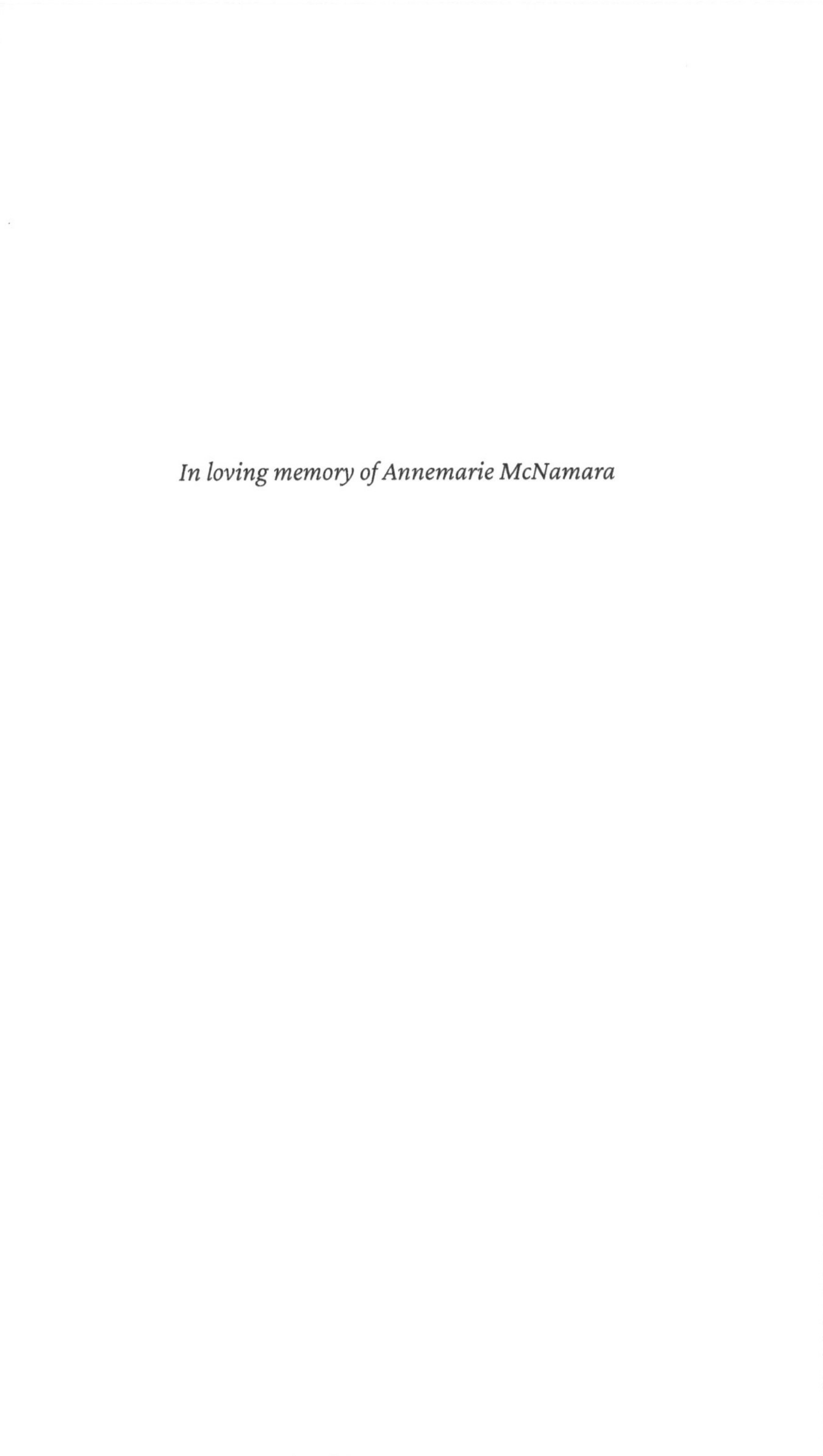

In loving memory of Annemarie McNamara

TRADEMARK ACKNOWLEDGEMENTS

- Sherlock - Conan Doyle Estate Ltd owns trademark for the name Sherlock (Holmes)
- Watson - Conan Doyle Estate Ltd owns trademark for the name Watson
- Jon Bon Jovi - trademark owned by Bon Jovi Productions, Inc
- Inspector Clouseau - rights owned by Metro-Goldwyn-Mayer
- Google - registered trademark owned by Google LLC, under parent company Alphabet, Inc
- Kemosabe - rights owned by NBC Universal
- Indiana Jones - trademark owned by Lucasfilm Ltd LLC
- Magnum PI - registered trademark for Universal City Studios LLC
- Groucho - registered trademark of Groucho Marx Productions
- Harpo - registered trademark of Groucho Marx Productions
- Agent 99 (Get Smart, CBS Media Ventures)
- Marvel - Walt Disney Company, Marvel Entertainment, Marvel Characters Inc
- Colonel Mustard Copyrighted by Hasbro
- Ghostbusters (movie) Columbia Pictures
- Crimson and Clover (song) Tommy James & The Shondells

- Captain Crunch (cereal brand) The Quaker Oats Company
- Pippi Longstocking ASTRID LINDGREN
- Dudley Do Right JMM Lee Properties
- It's My Life Bon Jovi Productions, Inc
- James Patterson Author
- Calvin Klein (designer brand) the Trustee of the Calvin Klein Trademark Trust
- Elton (musician) Elton John name mention only
- Village People (band) name mention only
- Gloria Gaynor, I Will Survive (artist and song) Gloria Gaynor
- Peter Pan (character) J.M. Barrie
- Saturday Night Fever (movie) Paramount Pictures Corporation
- Houdini (magician) name mention only
- Yoda (character from Star Wars) Lucasfilm Ltd. LLC
- Jedi (same) Lucasfilm Ltd. LLC
- Mr. Clean (brand) Procter & Gamble Company
- Grinch (character) Dr. Seuss
- Milky Way (candy bar) Mars, Incorporated
- Fester (character) from The Addams Family, Metro-Goldwyn-Mayer
- Let's stay together (Al Green)
- Blazing Saddles (Warner Brothers)
- Abba {Band Name, Abba}
- Zoom Video Communications, Inc
- Alfetta Alfa Romeo
- Bed Bath & Beyond Inc
- Toria Marie
- Marley (character) A Christmas Carol, Charles Dickens

- Cheshire Cat Alice's Adventures in Wonderland
  Lewis Carroll 1865

CHAPTER ONE

Babs: Emergency with Mother. Come quick!

I shook my head because, seriously, couldn't Babs, my intrepid twin sister, get our mother to the theater on time without it being a major catastrophe? My mom should already be standing at the front doors, two of her BFFs all set to lead her down the aisle. So, I had no idea what could have gone wrong. My best guess; our dear mother refused to wear a blindfold because she didn't particularly like surprises any more than I did. Either that or she thought the blindfold would ruin her blonde bob.

With a sigh, I rose to my feet. Then my phone buzzed again.

Babs: All's fine.

I sat back down.

"What is it?" Dani, my BFF, whispered beside me.

"Babs and her theatrics."

Dani grinned. "She gets it from your mom."

I chuckled just as an expectant hush took over the crowd seated in the rows and rows of red velvet upholstered chairs.

The audience was still, and everyone held their breath as my mom, blindfolded, gripped Hope's hand on one side and

Prudence's on the other and slowly walked toward the stage. Anticipation grew as she got closer. She had no clue what was happening—which was amazing because the entire town of Luckland was in on the surprise.

A few murmurs whispered throughout the theater as we waited for someone to lift the stage curtains and for Hope or Prudence to remove Mom's blindfold. Matilda, another of my mom's closest friends, stood just to the right of the stage, cueing someone on the other side to pull up the curtain.

Nothing happened. I glanced at Devon, my significant other, who sat on my other side from Dani. He narrowed his eyes.

Matilda lifted her arm and nodded once again. Still nothing. She frowned, then peeked around the curtain before she headed across the stage behind the long drapes. I guessed some poor teenager was about to get an earful. What I didn't expect was a blood-curdling scream.

Devon, Chief Marks when in uniform, jumped over the seats in front then hopped up on the stage, running off to the side where Matilda had screamed. Simon, his FBI buddy, was right behind him. My mother ripped off the blindfold and simply stared around in stunned silence. Martin O'Hara, local deputy sheriff and Prudence's husband, followed Devon and Simon to the back of the stage, and while other patrons stood and inched forward, I headed to my mom.

"What's happening?" she asked.

"Right now, I don't know, but I'm sure Devon can handle it," I said.

"That was Matilda's scream. Is she all right." Mom took a few steps toward the stage while Hope and Prudence appeared as confused as everyone else.

"This wasn't part of the show, I take it?" Dani asked as she came over.

"Of course not," Hope said, her brow furrowed.

"Ladies, gentlemen."

We all turned as Martin spoke from the stage.

"If you can all return to your seats for a moment. I'm afraid we'll have to cancel the show, and I'll need everyone here to give me their name as they leave." He descended the stage and strode to the front door, the previous murmurs now full cries of bewilderment.

I had no idea what they'd found backstage, but it spelled disaster.

It took half an hour, but eventually, everyone left. The only ones who remained inside were Devon, Simon, Martin, and the infamous Luckland Ladies, or the posse as I affectionately called my mother and her lifelong best friends.

I paused outside the front of the theater and took a breath. Thankfully, the night was clear, and the temperature wasn't too bad for June in Colorado. The gentle breeze was just cool enough to make the sweater I brought practical and not overkill.

I sighed. "Why is it nothing ever goes as planned in Luckland?"

Dani laughed beside me. "Because it's Luckland."

"Did you see what happened in there?" I asked her.

"No clue. Simon pushed me out the exit door before I could ask Matilda."

"Well damn. Guess we'll have to start texting."

I pulled up the Luckland Ladies group contact on my phone and fired away.

Me: What's going on?

We waited. Radio silence.

Me: Fine, we're coming back in.

I muttered as I typed. I must have muttered a bit too loud.

"No, Pip, you're not." Devon's voice sounded firm from behind my right ear.

I turned my head and looked up. "What happened? Why did Matilda scream? There aren't any bodies, are there?" I was really only kidding, but the look on his face was not filled with humor.

"Oh my god, there's a body?" Dani whispered, only to have Simon approach from the other side, shaking his head.

"Girls, go home. We'll see you there. There's nothing you can do for anyone here. Are we clear?" By Devon's tone, his inner authoritarian had taken control.

Dani and I looked at each other and shrugged. I reached up on my toes and gave Devon a quick kiss. After I grabbed Dani by the arm, we headed down Main Street toward home. Once we were out of hearing distance, I leaned close to her.

"As soon as we get home, we'll check the camera's uploads."

"You have pictures?" Dani looked at me, then smiled. "Of course you do, being the official town photographer."

"Yes, but I don't just have pictures. I have video."

I had set up a tripod a few feet from the right stage entrance, using a wide-angle lens, and primed the camera to capture video and stills of the moment Hope was to take off my mom's blindfold. I'd also set up a second camera on the catwalk above the rear of the stage. I was sure I'd caught whatever had happened behind the curtain.

Dani nodded approvingly. "Clever." She suddenly stopped as we approached my house. "Did you hear that?" she whispered.

"Hear what?" I asked just as quietly. I stopped breathing for a moment and listened. "I don't hear anything. What did you hear?"

"Like a twig or a branch breaking. It came from your front yard."

We stood on the sidewalk and watched my front yard for signs of movement. After a few moments of nothingness, I shrugged. "The noise was probably just Billy or Skye."

Devon's and my pygmy goats might be having a nighttime romp, though to do so was rare.

"We can check on them, but not dressed like this, I'm afraid. We're liable to step in something." I looked down for emphasis. I wore my new favorite emerald green dress and heels. Not my usual attire. I'd dressed to impress with my long auburn curls worn loose. Dani's coral cocktail dress worked in perfect harmony with her golden Caribbean skin tone and wavy sun-kissed hair. Also in heels, she looked at the muddy yard and grinned.

"Point taken, let's go inside."

Mystic Manor, an old, gothic-style house where occasionally strange things happened, was Devon's and my home. A gift from the ladies last year, Devon and I had spent months renovating it, and during those renovations, we'd witnessed several hauntings, like the Native American woman who had ironically appeared in the middle of a séance the ladies had held to find out what could be causing the hauntings at Mystic Manor and other happenings that were going on in their lives at the time.

Morgan and her boyfriend Hunter had eventually laid claim to the hauntings, stating they were filming a paranormal movie. I still didn't believe they'd faked everything that had happened, and right about then, the house had an eerie aura surrounding it, though that could be because our streetlamp was out—which was odd because Luckland's council had recently fitted LED bulbs to all the streetlamps.

I shivered, though it wasn't the house's aura that caused my skin to tighten and the hairs on the back of my neck to stand on end. Something didn't feel right. I turned and looked out onto the darkened street, which was when another snap cracked through the whisper-quiet of the late spring air.

Dani and I whipped around, then strode purposefully up the walkway to the house, where I quickly used the electronic opener on my phone Devon had installed. As soon as we got inside, I flipped on the lights to the foyer, shut the door, locked it, then leaned against it for good measure.

I turned to Dani. "Is it me, or does something feel off to you?"

"Yeah. I just texted Simon. He's on his way."

"Good idea." I wasn't surprised she'd instinctively thought of Simon to come and check outside, though if I questioned Dani about the relationship building between them for over a year, she'd deny anything was going on. They were thirty going on thirteen when it came to acknowledging they had the hots for each other, but I found it funny they'd both decided to come to Luckland for a vacation at the same time—and stay with Devon and me.

I pulled off my shoes, then wiggled my toes. Dani did the same before she pulled me by the arm and headed to the kitchen. "We can check on the goats later. Let's see that video, Pippa. Come on."

Of the same mind, I grabbed my laptop from its perch on the counter, sat at the table, then fired it up while she nabbed a couple of hard ciders from the fridge.

I began to scroll through the video a few frames at a time until a shadow caught my eye. I slowed the video and studied it.

"Lois Thorpe! Holy bat burgers, Dani. Look at this."

"Lois? Town gossip and resident busybody Lois? What about her?"

"She's the reason Matilda screamed."

CHAPTER TWO

"Was it natural causes?" I asked as soon as Devon came in, followed by Simon.

"Was what natural causes?" Devon frowned. "What do you know, and who told you?" He stood tall, legs apart, hands on his hips. He'd dressed for a night on the town in a pair of well-worn jeans with a button-down white cotton shirt, sleeves pushed up, looking hot as hell—and now annoyed as hell. His aquamarine eyes flared as he blew a lock of beautiful chestnut brown hair off his forehead.

"Before you get yourself riled up, come see what I have." I beckoned him by crooking my finger and smiling. Devon strode over and stood behind me.

"There, see it?" I froze the image at the moment when Lois collapsed. "That, Kemosabe, is how I know things."

"Humph," he muttered as he grabbed a chair and sat. Simon headed to the fridge, grabbed a beer for each of them, and returned to the table before grabbing the remaining chair. The thing about Devon and Simon was that they were big guys. Well over six feet tall, broad, and, as I liked to say, handsome devils. Simon was exotic, with his creole caramel complexion and movie star good looks. Devon was more Hollywood-style cowboy cop. Together, the two were an explosive combination.

"So, was it?" I asked.

"Was it what?"

"Was it natural, or do we have a killer on the loose in Luckland?"

"Pretty sure Lois died of natural causes. No signs of foul play. So, you can rein in that imagination of yours," Simon said.

"Lois didn't seem sick to me at the town picnic last week," Dani said. She drained her cider and pushed her chair back. I figured she was headed to get another, but Simon quickly stood.

"I'll get it. Stay," he said.

Dani seemed about to protest, but she relented, a tiny crease marring her brow. I glanced from Dani to Simon and back again. One day they'd get their act together, and I couldn't wait for that day.

"People die suddenly all the time, Dani," Simon said as he returned to the table.

"This is Luckland, Simon. Nothing is ever as it seems," I said as a reminder of the odd things that had happened in town over the past year. "I hope you at least order an autopsy."

"Well, that will depend on the coroner. They'll order one if Lois didn't suffer any medical issues or hadn't seen a doctor recently. If they order one, her sister Louise *could* object, but I'm sure she'd want to find out what happened. We'll be meeting with the coroner and Louise in the morning." Devon looked thoughtful for a moment. "Dani's right, you know. Last week Louise and Lois did the potato sack race. Lois was in fine form. For an older lady."

"Where's the body now?" I asked.

"The medical examiner took Lois to his office." Devon slid

his hand to the back of my neck and tapped his fingers—he was thinking of something.

I was busily thinking of more questions to ask when phones started buzzing. I looked at mine and frowned. "Babs says to hightail it over to the café."

Devon held up his phone. "My mom basically said the same thing."

"When you say basically, you mean what precisely?" I asked.

"Her text said 'Café, now, bring everyone.'"

I looked at Dani. "Mama's says '*ven al cafe y mueve tu tresero.*'"

I chuckled. "Translation, please?"

"Well, let's see. Literally, it means 'Come to the café and shake your butt.'" Dani grinned.

Simon laughed. "Gotta love Mama Rosa. I think she meant move your ass, am I right?"

"Either that or it's pole dancing night at the Blue Sky," Dani remarked.

"On that note, shall we?" Devon stood and held out a hand, color highlighting his cheeks. I loved it when he blushed. When we were kids, he always poked and teased me, making me blush —which wasn't hard with me being a freckled-faced redhead. As adults, seeing him blush was karmic.

We headed to the front door, where Dani and I slipped on our shoes, groaning a little at the discomfort. As Devon opened the front door to leave, I stopped short and pulled on his hand.

"The light, you fixed it?"

"Fixed it? No, haven't touched it."

"It was off when we came home."

"And we heard noises too," Dani said, backing me up.

"I'll take a look," Simon said quietly as he slipped by us and headed down the steps to the walkway. He paused every so often, looking about and listening. When he got to the lamp, he lifted the glass housing, then unscrewed the bulb. The sidewalk around him went dark. About a minute later, the light came on again.

"Seems to be fine," he called out. "Let's go before your mothers send the rescue squad."

Main Street in Luckland wasn't all that big, about six blocks long and lined with historic frontier-style buildings—charming for tourists and convenient for those who resided there. Devon and I lived just past the east end of Main Street, while the café sat at the west end. Nobody had technically said it was an emergency, so we walked, though my pinched toes signaled a ride would have been nicer.

I grabbed Devon's hand, still feeling as if something was off. Last year, I'd received a threatening postcard, and soon after, I had the strange sensation of being watched. I felt that sensation again now. Devon didn't seem concerned, nor did Simon. Dani, however, kept glancing over at me. She felt it too.

Entering the bright and airy café, I focused on the posse who all sat at one of the large, counter-height tables Hope and her wife Marcy had recently installed. It was all the rage, apparently. Hope and Marcy owned the café, which they'd moved from their old location to what was once the bakery, attached to the Inn, which they'd also purchased.

They were seated at the new table with my mom, Kate, Dani's mother, Rosa, Devon's mother, Matilda, and Prudence. Babs leaned against the doorway to the kitchen, looking a bit pale. Actually, she looked frightened. My dad had hunkered down in the back with the other spouses, Tom, Trey, and Martin —otherwise now known collectively as the *boys*. That explained why Devon and Simon beelined for the back, leaving Dani and me to face the posse.

"What's this?" I pointed to the board lying in the middle of their table. Each of the women had markers, and they were all scribbling things and marking arrows everywhere. Each of them also had a frosted glass in front of them, with two pitchers of margaritas at the ready.

"We're trying to figure out what happened to dearly departed Loish," Prudence announced.

"You're all three sheets to the wind, aren't you?" I asked, just noticing the additional empty pitchers in the center of the table. I sighed, looked around the table, and raised an eyebrow. "None of you liked Lois."

"Well, shush your mouth, young lady. It's wrong to speak ill of the dead."

Just when I thought the night couldn't get any stranger, I turned toward the voice coming from the front entrance and watched Hilda Feingold, Marcy's aunt, breeze in. Now the nightmare was complete. The nearly ninety-one-year-old author of cozy mysteries grabbed the last remaining chair, then reached over to grab a marker from the Styrofoam cup they'd placed in the middle. After pulling the cap off the marker with her teeth, she leaned in and drew an arrow from what I thought was supposed to be a body but resembled more of a stick figure, and the back of what appeared to be the stage. I had to tilt my head sideways a few times to figure it out.

"Lois was here. Whoever did it came in from here." Hilda waved her arm about to illustrate her point.

"Whoever did what?" I asked. I must have been a little slow on the uptake because it took me a few seconds to realize what she was talking about. When I had, I almost groaned aloud. Trust the posse to automatically assume someone murdered Lois.

"Well, I think that frozen heart of hers just gave out." Hope sighed and swayed on her stool.

Spinning stools were a very bad idea. Concerned the women

really needed to sit lower to the ground, in chairs, I glanced around the café. However, every seat was taken.

"I'm going to need all your car keys," I said firmly, holding out my hand.

"We came afoot," Matilda said.

"Afoot?" I tried to stop myself from rolling my eyes as Dani bit back a grin.

"Maybe Louise did it," my mother whispered. "You know, I heard those two sisters were jealous of each other. Scratched each other's eyes out once."

Babs came over and glanced down at the board before she nervously scanned the regular customers. "From where I was sitting, I saw someone go out the back," she said quietly.

My camera hadn't caught anyone leaving the back of the theater, and I frowned. "Could have been anyone, Babs."

Hilda shook her head. "I bet it was the killer."

CHAPTER THREE

THE RAIN PATTER ON THE WINDOW FIRST THING SATURDAY MORNING had me pulling the covers up over my head and reaching for Devon. Rain meant only two things for me: no morning hike and no gardening, though not gardening was a given. I had a black thumb. Curling up with Devon for a few extra minutes was just the way to start my day—finding his side of the bed cold and empty was not.

The soft murmur of voices and the heavenly aroma of coffee floated upstairs. Perhaps I'd overstayed my welcome in bed. I pushed the curtain aside on the front-facing window, just to verify it was indeed a rainy day, and frowned. "Heads up!" I yelled as I made my way down the stairs. "Incoming!"

I'd caught a glimpse of Louise Thorpe climbing out of a sedan parked in my driveway. I didn't believe she'd ever been to my house, and I saw no reason for her to be here now. If she needed Devon's help, all she had to do was call him. Everyone in Luckland knew that dialing the police rang straight to his cell.

As soon as I got to the bottom of the stairs, the bell rang, and I immediately regretted my decision to install it. I'd thought the gong-like sound was fun at the time—very in keeping with the gothic vibe we had going. Now though, the bell echoed through the house and continued to resonate as I opened the door.

"Good morning, Pippa. I'm here to see Devon." Not waiting for me to invite her in, she entered and shook out her umbrella on my newly sanded and stained floors. Considering the circumstances, I made an allowance for her rudeness.

When Devon approached, he gave my shoulder a squeeze. I understood completely—escape to the kitchen and leave him to handle it. The life of living with a law enforcement officer required an uncanny ability to communicate without words.

I slipped off to the kitchen and joined Simon at the table. Dani, a night owl, tended to rise at the stroke of noon unless she was on a dive.

"Coffee?" Simon lifted his mug.

"Please."

He rose, fetched me a mug, and poured me a generous amount of coffee. I swirled a little cream in it, took a sip, and sighed. "What on earth is in this? It's heavenly."

"A little secret from home."

"Which is?"

"Chicory root. Now you're gonna have to swear to keep it secret, Pip."

"You know I can't. Keeping secrets is not in me. For you, though, I'll try to keep the news local." I took another sip of coffee, then focused back on Simon. "So, when do you head out? Not that I'm trying to get rid of you. I'm just curious. You must have another assignment somewhere?" He and Devon were always off on mysterious assignments. Devon had allegedly retired from the FBI, but I sometimes doubted it.

"Funny you should ask. I was thinking of sticking around

for a bit and taking advantage of the gorgeous scenery." His grin told me he spoke about more than the Rocky Mountains.

"And how long will you be staying?"

Before he could answer, Louise's voice rose from the foyer, apparently not happy.

"You will *not* butcher my sister."

I stood and tiptoed over to the kitchen door to put my ear against it.

"Now, Louise, an autopsy would tell us how your sister died. Don't you want to know?" Devon asked, his voice calm.

"Doc said it was heart failure. That's good enough for me." From the sound of her, Louise seemed to be panicking.

"He can't know what killed her without an autopsy, and she was only fifty-nine with no prior history of illness except a little high blood pressure."

"My mother died at fifty-nine. I will too. It's a family thing. Leave it alone. Send her over to Mort's, and he'll take care of it."

Mort's was Mort Steinberg, Luckland's funeral director and mortician.

Our front door slammed. With me not being that fast in the morning, when Devon pushed open the swinging door from the other side, he bopped me in the nose.

"Ow!" I rubbed my nose and frowned.

Devon smirked while shaking his head. "Isn't that what you like to call karma, Pip?" He quickly gave me a kiss to make it better, which helped. Granted, if I hadn't been eavesdropping, it wouldn't have happened.

I sat back at the table and took another sip of my coffee. "So, Louise doesn't want an autopsy. That's kind of odd, isn't it? I mean, like you said, without one, no one will know how Lois died."

Devon grimaced. "I'll talk to the ME and see if he thinks one is warranted. I don't like my chances, however."

"Don't you think Lois's death is suspicious?" I asked.

"Not really, though I will look into finding out if anyone has a motive for murder."

"Money," I said. "That's always a motive."

"Yes, Red. I'm aware," Devon replied with a chuckle.

I was sure Devon and Simon would be aware of plenty of motives. "What I don't get is why the posse would allow Lois, of all people. to volunteer for Mom's big surprise. Lois and my mom were practically mortal enemies. They've never liked each other, so why would Lois be a part of the event?"

"Good question. My mom chattered on non-stop about 'Kate's Comeback,' as she called it, and never mentioned Lois once."

"'Kate's Comeback?'" Simon asked, confused. Though we'd invited him to the grand opening of our new community theater, we hadn't explained why Mom's friends had renovated it.

"Short version or long version?" I asked him.

"Medium, please," Simon replied, grinning.

"My mom always planned on leaving Luckland someday for the bright lights of Broadway. She had it all planned out. She was going to attend the theater arts program at a university just north of New York City. She'd auditioned, and they'd accepted her."

"She must have been quite talented," Simon remarked.

"Still is, so don't let her fool you. However, that's when things went south. The summer after her high school gradua-tion, my grandparents went to New Mexico for an annual hot air balloon festival. The balloon crashed, and they didn't survive."

I'd never met them, but it still left me sad when I spoke of their accident. I had only one grandparent growing up. My dad's mom, and she died when I was young. I shook off my melancholy and continued.

"After that, my mom went to live at Hope's and attended community college in Denver. Anyway, my mom's birthday is coming up. As you know, for Matilda's sixtieth birthday last year, they gave her Trey." I smiled as I remembered that chaotic plan. "This year, they decided it was my mom's turn for a big surprise. When the owners of the old, run-down theater decided to demolish it, Matilda, Pru, and Hope stepped in and bought it. They decided it was time for my mom to have her very own playhouse. They've spent months fixing it up. Hope wrote a special play just for opening night, Marcy and Prudence built the sets with the help of some local art students, and Matilda coordinated it all. Last night was supposed to be a huge surprise to unveil the theater renovations, put on a play, and give Mom the keys to the queendom."

"It's a shame your mom didn't get the surprise the ladies wanted for her," Devon said. "They probably had a fit that Lois's death blew it all out the water."

"Why do I feel like Lois was a bit of a pariah?" Simon asked. "I know you all aren't that callous, but it sure seems like nobody is mourning her."

I sighed and shrugged. "Lois Thorpe was the ultimate town gossip. I don't know all the details, but when our moms and the others were young, Lois made their lives miserable. As they got older, it got worse."

"Remember that case we worked in Boston, Simon? The Wicked Widow?" Devon asked.

"No way. Lois was a Wicked Widow?" Simon widened his eyes and shook his head.

"Explain, please. Who is the Wicked Widow."

Simon grinned. "Devon got to play the man about town. Undercover, of course. His assignment was to take this woman out for dinner. Her code name was the Wicked Widow. Devon spent two hours trapped with her. Her voice was high-pitched, and all she did was describe every single diner and their secrets."

Devon rolled his eyes, which was unusual. "Finally, she pointed to the table next to us and told me the woman sitting there was having an affair with the man at the table behind us. Next thing you know, there's a fistfight at our table, the *Wicked Widow* disappears, and I end up with a black eye."

"I certainly never heard that story before, but yeah, Lois was that bad. She had a chip on her shoulder the size of Mount Rushmore."

"Why?" Simon asked. "What was her story?"

"That, my friend, is a tale for another day, as we must be off." Devon stood and nodded at Simon.

I sighed in disappointment as the two disappeared. Alone, I had nothing to do unless I cleaned the kitchen or woke Dani. Of the two choices, waking Dani headed my list.

CHAPTER FOUR

THE RAIN CONTINUED MONDAY. NOT A GOOD OMEN.

Devon and I, along with Simon and Dani, arrived fifteen minutes early to Lois's funeral and took seats in the back of the Upward Bound Room, so named because Mort had gone all out and painted an alfresco on the ceiling. Not a blue sky with clouds and a gate to heaven, however. When mourners sat down and looked up, they saw the Milky Way. When he'd finished the painting, I had the privilege of photographing it, and I asked him why he'd painted stars. He said none of us knew where we were headed, just that we hoped it was up.

Mort had placed freshly printed programs on everyone's seat, complete with an advert on the back for his services—which, considering he was the only game in town when residents met their maker, was a little redundant. Louise already sat down front, sniffling quite loudly and dramatically. At least she wasn't wailing. The women also sat in the front, each with a white rose in their hair after I'd informed them peace lilies didn't work so well as a hair accessory because they were poisonous.

As the other town residents filtered in, I noticed a few unfamiliar faces. I could only surmise the Thorpes had some out-of-town relatives. I didn't know much about the sisters, other than they grew up with the posse in Luckland. I made a mental note to explore the Thorpes' history because, like most families in Luckland, they were probably descendants of the pioneers who arrived and put down roots after the four original founders. The four Irish immigrants who founded and built the town in the 1850s were gold-seekers. Rumor had it they found gold, and a legend was born. So now, even more than a hundred and seventy years later, the town had a target on its back for gold diggers—which was why any unfamiliar faces had everyone taking notice. What no one seemed to know was that the founders *had* found gold. Late last year, Devon and I had unearthed a record from the 1850s of a registered, patented lode claim, proof the founders had discovered gold but not how much or whether they'd dug it up.

Granted, having strangers in our midst wasn't uncommon. Luckland didn't just have one legend; it had two. The gold, and our wandering ghosts. It was said Luckland was built on sacred Native American ground, and once a year we celebrated Founders' Day to pay tribute to our ancestors and to perform a ritual that kept the spirits of those buried beneath and around the town appeased. The ritual, of course, was performed by the illustrious posse, who were also direct descendants of the original four.

I leaned close to Devon. "I didn't realize the funeral would be quite so soon. I assume the coroner didn't find anything suspicious?"

"He decided not to do an autopsy, and as I couldn't see anything obvious to point to murder, I had to accede to his expertise. However, he did take a blood sample to do further tests."

I nodded and squeezed Devon's hand. I didn't like funerals, but then I supposed nobody did.

"Do you think they have anything planned?" I whispered as I nodded to the posse. I had a horrible suspicion they intended to stage some kind of commotion in revenge for all the nasty deeds Lois had enacted on them. I hoped they wouldn't stoop so low, but Lois's actions had hurt them, and I wouldn't put it past them.

"I have no idea, but don't worry. If it gets ugly, we'll cause a distraction. I've got it covered."

I leaned in and gave him a quick kiss. "I hope so, Dev." I did. I really hoped we weren't in for another of the Luckland Ladies' fiascos.

The casket sat on a raised platform, almost like a stage, draped in flowers with photos of Lois on top. It wasn't an open casket, thankfully. Mort stood in front and cleared his throat.

He said a few nice words about Lois, then Louise got up and did the same, followed by a succession of neighbors. It appeared the ladies had opted not to speak, and I breathed a tremendous sigh of relief, though I doubted we were out of the woods. The burial at the cemetery would give the ladies one more opportunity to screw things up.

As everyone stood to leave, I quickly zeroed in on the ladies who, while dressed in traditional black, all wore capri wide-leg slacks with a wrap tunic. As they stood, they each swung up an arm, synchronized, and placed big, floppy black hats on their heads. Then they marched out. Devon and I quickly scooted behind them to follow. Once outside, they placed a pair of enormous dark sunglasses over their eyes. It wasn't sunny. It was drizzling. It was bizarre. They all looked like they were auditioning for a b-list movie.

"What are they up to?" I whispered to Devon, whose expression turned watchful. Tense.

"I don't know, but we can't let them out of our sight. Not for a second." He frowned, then took my hand and pulled me toward the car, conveniently though illegally parked. We got in, and he waited until Matilda's SUV pulled away from the curb, then he eased us into the procession behind them.

We pulled through the imposing wrought iron gates of the small cemetery located just outside of town, and I shivered. Driving along the dirt path through a cemetery on a rainy day was incredibly creepy. The trees casting shadows over the grave sites sent all kinds of images through my brain, so I focused on the huge white canopy over Lois's freshly dug plot. Mort was nothing if not prepared. There were a handful of chairs I assumed were reserved for the family.

Devon grabbed an umbrella from the back seat and came around to the passenger side. Then he opened the door and the umbrella simultaneously. Ever the gentleman. We walked along with everyone else who'd parked as we had, then stood to the outer edge of the canopy, allowing the elders to occupy the chairs.

As Mort electronically lowered the casket into the ground, Louise began sobbing uncontrollably. She was the only one. Several people standing behind her reached over her shoulder with tissues dangling. On the other side of the dirt pit, all in a row, stood the Luckland Ladies. Hats on, sunglasses on, with very odd expressions. From left to right was Matilda, tall, lithe, and imperial, then my mother, petite and fairy-like. Next was Prudence, curvy and the life of the party, followed by Hope, the quintessential neat and tidy librarian, and Marcy, filled with exuberance and mystical charm. Capping the row off was Dani's mom, Rosa, the exotic Caribbean queen. I assumed Hilda had stayed at home, and I could only hope the others would just let Lois rest in peace and not attempt to disparage the poor woman.

When Mort handed Louise the symbolic shovel, she stood then jammed the shovel into the pile of dirt. With a wild swing, she whooshed the dirt into the pit. I looked at the women, who now held hands. They were going to do something. I just knew it. Their men stood behind them. I sincerely hoped the men were there not for support but to avert dangerous behavior.

When the ladies all took one step forward, I closed my eyes and held my breath—then thanked the ever-lovin' lord above when my dad's phone rang. Really rang. He was the only one I knew who didn't use special ringtones. Everyone stopped and watched as he answered it.

"Son of a bitch, they took my babies!"

CHAPTER FIVE

"Take it from me, we need a plan." Hilda leaned back and looked at everyone gathered at the extended table in the back of the Blue Sky Café. "As the resident crime expert, I can tell you we need to lay out the facts, analyze them, and plan our next steps."

Marcy frowned. "Aunt Hilda, we all appreciate your help, but we don't have any facts. All we know is the mechanic went up to inspect Colin's Alfa Romeo race cars and found the two of them missing."

Hilda shook her head. "You see, Marcy, that's where you're wrong. We have many facts. Now, bring out that board and those markers, and let's get to work."

Dani and I looked at each other.

"We should have followed Devon and Simon up to the barn," Dani said quietly.

"Agreed. Did you know Devon learned to drive in one of Dad's Alfettas? He was going to teach me to drive one. Now I won't get the chance."

"You don't think your dad will get them back?"

"I doubt it. They're worth a fortune."

"The question is, who took them?" my mother asked, butting in on my conversation.

I had my suspicions, but I wasn't sure whether mentioning it would help. Then again… I checked to make sure no one in the café could overhear. "Hunter Jackson."

"Morgan's boyfriend?" Hope asked curiously. "Why do you say that?"

"Because not only is he a stunt driver, a construction worker, an undergraduate in Astronomy, has a Master's in Metallurgical Engineering, and a PhD in Mining Engineering, he's also a race car driver." Well, that certainly shut them all up. I wanted to smile but couldn't because I really was upset about the missing cars. My dad's babies.

"Pippa O'Leary, you've been keeping secrets," Prudence said.

"No, I've been protecting information I had gathered during an investigation," I said proudly. I had actually impressed myself that I'd not told anyone what I'd learned about Morgan's hottie boyfriend. "It wasn't relevant until now."

"After you found out he'd crashed that car at your house, why didn't you tell us about his degree in mining? That means that whole paranormal filming thing was a sham," Hope said. "He was here for the gold."

My mother shook her head. "Look, we don't know that. It's possible the film company, BMC I think it was, hired Hunter randomly and coincidentally."

Hilda sat up. "It's also possible the film company is a front. Perhaps whoever owns it knew about the legend, and they hired Hunter to look for the gold."

"But why steal the cars?" Dani asked. "If he was trying to find Luckland's gold, why do something that draws attention to him?"

"So, maybe it's not him after all," Babs said quietly.

"Okay, Babs, I'm game. Who do you think took them?" I asked.

"Same person who killed Lois."

I frowned. "What makes you think anyone killed Lois?"

She shrugged. "I don't know exactly, but something tells me she didn't die of a heart attack or whatever. I saw someone run out the back of the theater, and no one has admitted to doing so. Don't you think that's odd?" What was odd was Babs taking an interest in a mystery. Normally, she tried to keep clear of the ladies' mayhem and madness.

Hilda stood and grabbed her umbrella, waving it in the air. "So, in order to figure out who stole the cars, we need to figure out who killed Lois. Let's go, ladies. I've got an idea. First stop, the Playhouse." With that, she pointed the umbrella at the door and started making her way toward it. Slowly. At her age, she was fairly mobile, miraculously so, but still wasn't a speed demon.

The rest of the women all stood at once and, throwing their hats and sunglasses back on, also marched out. Dani, Babs, and I remained seated. It was one thing to offer conjecture, but none of us wanted in on whatever the older generation was up to. I was more interested in what the boys were doing. The barn they'd headed to was a massive structure located in the mountains. Until recently, I'd had no idea the barn and its contents existed. My dad had stored his two classic race cars in there for years. I visualized the boys standing in the empty building, trying to determine how the cars had disappeared.

"Considering the weather, whoever stole the cars must have left tracks in the ground. The drive to the barn turns into a semi-paved dirt road." I grinned. "Perfect for my Jeep."

Dani grinned back, but Babs shook her head. She wasn't the adventurous sort.

"Come on, Babs, we need to see what's going on for

ourselves. While the ladies hunt for Lois's killer, we'll go help hunt for the car thief."

Reluctantly, she nodded. "Okay, but only because Tom has Leah's playgroup right now. Those little girls can be a terror." She smiled then. "Reminds me of you when we were four."

"You mean us, don't you?" I replied with maybe a little snark in my tone.

Babs snickered. "No, I was always the good one. You were the one with your pants on fire all the time."

"What does that even mean?" I asked, laughing along with her.

"Never mind. If we're going to do this, let's get this show on the road. Finn?" Babs called over to our favorite Blue Sky server, though now he was the manager of the café and the attached Luckland Inn.

Finn came over, a to-go cup in hand with what I assumed was whatever Babs routinely ordered.

"Let me guess, a vanilla chai with almond milk?"

"Don't knock it. It's got more caffeine than that French press crap."

"Girls, behave," Dani said as she stood. "Let's go. I'm driving."

I handed her the keys. "Fine, but you have to wash the Jeep afterward. Rules of the road."

"I call shotgun," Babs announced, which forced me into the back seat, my butt bouncing on every bump in the narrow winding mountain road. As we pulled off the road onto the dirt and gravel path leading to the meadow and the barn, Dani thankfully slowed. There were several cars parked ahead, which I assumed belonged to Devon, Simon, and the boys. The only one missing was Martin. He had to stay behind when Devon left town. Technically, Martin wasn't a Luckland cop, he was a county deputy, but they all watched each other's backs.

We parked enough away from the barn so we wouldn't cover up any tracks, though there was only one road in and out, so technically, just arriving tampered with evidence. The guys hovered close to the ground, and I assumed they were measuring and photographing whatever evidence the thieves had left.

"Any luck?" I called out as we approached.

"Yeah, we've got it covered. Stay back there so you don't step on anything," Devon replied.

Babs immediately lifted her foot to check the bottom of her boot.

"What are you doing?" I asked.

"Seeing if I stepped in anything."

"He's talking about the... Oh, never mind." I unslung my pack and pulled out a vinyl blanket to sit on and a bottle of wine to enjoy while we watched the men work.

"Is he here?" Dani whispered as she spotted me eyeing the trees. I'd told her about the ghost I'd seen last year of an old man who had sat at the base of a tree, whittling a piece of wood. The ghost had winked at me—just the way Devon did. At some point, I'd wondered if the ghost was an ancestor of Devon's. It certainly wouldn't have surprised me, though I had questioned what he was doing all the way up here and not in Luckland, where all the ancestors were purported to be buried. Maybe something kept him in the mountains and not in town.

"No." Odd how I sounded disappointed.

CHAPTER SIX

"Hey! I think I found something!" Trey jogged out of the barn waving his hand and holding what appeared to be a piece of paper.

Devon stood from his crouched position. "What do you have there?"

Whenever I heard Devon speak to Trey, I waited to hear if Devon used Trey's name or if Devon would call Trey Dad. I had done the same when Devon learned Matilda, who he'd known his whole life as Aunt Matilda, was his mother. It hadn't taken him long to call her Mom. I was still waiting with him and Trey. It was totally frustrating that Devon simply didn't call Trey anything most of the time. At least when I was around.

Trey handed over the paper, and Devon perused it before he frowned. He handed it to Simon, who had the same reaction. He handed it back. My dad stepped over and held out his hand—obviously annoyed to be the last one to look at it.

Devon came over to our little spectator section, still frowning. "We're wrapping this up. We all need to go."

"What was on the paper?" I asked. I wasn't going anywhere without that information.

"It was a message. They want the map."

"Who wants what map? You mean the founders' map?" Babs asked.

"Yes, the founders' map, and whoever took the cars wants the map," Devon muttered. "Now let's go. Okay?"

He was crankier than usual. Something bugged him, but there were too many others around for me to find out what. "Pip, you ride with me. Simon will drive your Jeep back."

"Dani's driving," I said. "They'll have to settle that one themselves." That at least got a smirk out of him.

We headed to Luckland's brand-new official PD vehicle, an SUV that had arrived the week before and in which I'd yet to ride. I looked forward to it. He had the car in gear and well on our way while I still tried to figure out how to adjust the seat after Simon had clearly ridden in it. I felt like a mouse in a giant Ferris wheel.

"Need some help there, Pip?" Devon laughed. The nerve.

"No, thank you, I've got it. Maybe you can program it for me. I heard these new models do that. You have user profiles."

"That's for the driver, which is me, not the passenger. Sorry." He still smiled, which was good. Something had really been bothering him though, and I aimed to find out what.

"Okay, Devon, spill it. What had your undies in a twist back there?"

"The note. It said, 'give us the star map, or the cars will meet their maker.' Star map, Pip. Not map." Devon gnawed on his lip. "Whoever took the cars knows what kind of map the founders used to get to Luckland. They must also know the map at the town hall is a fake. That's not your average gold digger, is it?"

"It has to be Hunter, doesn't it? He and Morgan know the town hall map is a fake. I mentioned him to the ladies, and Hilda suggested the film company hired Hunter to look for the gold, but then Dani questioned why he'd steal the cars because doing so would draw attention to him. Obviously, stealing the cars is linked to the gold, so it has to be Hunter. He's an astronomical miner after all."

"A what?" Devon laughed out loud, and I smiled, glad to have lightened his mood.

"I'd like to know why anyone would think we'd hand over a map that could be worth millions for cars that are only worth thousands. We know the founders discovered gold because of the registered claim, but there's no record of where the gold is, and I doubt the map leads to the exact location. It just leads to Luckland, doesn't it?" Devon had the original map, which he'd taken from behind the picture in his mom's house, and though he'd never outright admitted it, I knew. Where he'd put it was another matter.

He smiled. "I have no idea where the map leads. Let's say whoever knows of the map also knows of the registered gold claim and assumes one leads to the other, but you're right to ask why anyone would think the ladies would hand over the original map for those cars, or even why anyone thinks the ladies have the map. It doesn't make sense."

"If the thief knows the map at town hall is a fake, it doesn't take a genius to figure the last descendants of the four founders could have the original. Does the note say where the exchange is supposed to take place?"

Devon sighed. "Nope, so I assume we'll get another note or a call at some stage, but don't worry about that. I'll handle it. You and Dani need to keep an eye on the women. I have a bad feeling they're up to no good."

"How do you know they're up to anything?" I asked, careful to keep my tone neutral.

"A hunch. Normally, they would have followed you up here." He eyed me suspiciously. "Wait, you know what they're up to. Where are they now? Come on, out with it."

I studied his face for a moment, trying to determine if he was in a forgiving mood. "Last time I saw them, they were discussing poor Lois's demise. They're concerned her death wasn't entirely natural."

Devon groaned. "They've been reading too many of those TK Moreaux books."

"Hilda did mention she was working on a new manuscript."

Devon raised a brow. "Murder at the Playhouse?"

"Funny boy." I laughed and shook my head. I loved this alone time with him. Since Simon and Dani had been staying with us, we hadn't had much privacy. Devon must have had the same thought because he reached over and took my hand, holding on to it as we headed down the mountain. Between Lois's untimely death, our houseguests, and the missing race cars, I was pretty sure we weren't going to have much time to ourselves until everything settled down.

At the Manor, several cars already sat out front. Simon had beaten us back, but my dad's truck and Matilda's SUV were also there. We pulled into the driveway, and I leaned back and shut my eyes, willing them all to go away.

No such luck. As soon as we stepped out of Devon's vehicle, the ladies and their entourage descended on us like a flock of birds and followed us right into the house. I waved one arm in the air, muttering, "Make yourself at home, why don't you."

They all did. In the sunroom. Devon and I headed straight for the kitchen.

I wrapped my arms around him. More for me than him. When my anxiety got too high, I would rest my head on his chest and listen to his heartbeat. Worked every time. He enfolded me with his warmth, and we just stood there quietly for a moment, gathering our wits. When he finally eased back and looked down at me, he smiled.

"You get the drinks, and I'll get the food," he said softly. "We got this."

I hoped so. Sometimes, the ladies were just too much. I did as he said and poured a large bottle of pre-mixed margarita into a pitcher, threw some glasses onto a tray, and carried it out to our impromptu gathering.

A moment later, Devon brought in snacks, and we sat in our brand-new double-sized easy chair and waited for someone to start the show. Finally, when I supposed Devon could take it no longer, he cleared his throat. He absentmindedly ran his fingers through my hair—something he only did when pondering something significant.

"So, can I ask what you've all been up to?" Devon looked at the ladies, all seated at the card table. "Mom? Care to indulge me?"

Uh-oh. Devon knew something. I turned to look at him. He raised his brows and flipped his phone over so I could see his text messages. Martin had told him the ladies were in the Playhouse. Damn.

"How about I start you off? Did you find anything significant in your search of the theater?" Devon asked.

"Now that you mention it, Devon, we just might have," Hilda said, breaking the women's silence.

"We all know you think Lois dropped dead because it was time for her to go," Prudence said a bit flippantly.

"But really, if it was her time, then we're all in trouble. She was younger than us," Matilda said.

"Which is why we are all quite sure it was murder," Hope whispered.

"And we can prove it." My mother held up a small slip of paper.

"What do you have there, Kate?" Simon asked.

"It's a receipt."

Devon stood, then strode over to the card table. "Let me see that, and where did you get this?"

"Never mind that. She spent over two hundred dollars at Bed Bath & Beyond, which means she was expecting company," my mom said.

I sat forward. "How does one equate to the other?"

"Well, it's obvious. Brand-new towels for the guest bathroom, new crockery and cutlery, and one of those fancy cake plates."

I didn't particularly see how any of the items necessarily meant Lois expected company or that the towels were destined for the guest bathroom, but perhaps my mom's theory had merit.

"Louise didn't mention anything about Lois having company recently," Devon said.

"Sisters don't always know *everything*," Babs replied, shaking her head. "Maybe Lois had a beau. Maybe she was on one of those dating sites, like the one Matilda was going to go on. What was that called, lonely hearts hookup?"

I had to laugh. Babs hardly ever cracked a good joke. At least, I hoped she was joking.

"What's that? Tillie? You were on a dating site?" Trey gave her a quick kiss, which might have been him reassuring himself those days were behind her.

"I'll follow up on the receipt, but in the meantime, let's talk about why you're all here—the note someone left at the barn," Devon said.

"We don't have the map," Matilda said. "Someone stole it, remember?"

Devon had the good grace not to argue that she shouldn't have hidden it behind a picture in her home. He also didn't admit he was the one who'd "stolen" it. I wasn't sure he'd ever admit to that transgression. He had his reasons, I supposed.

Probably because if he confessed he had the map, the women would demand he hand it back.

"Do you have any other copies? Kate said she had a copy in one of the shoeboxes that went missing."

"That we still haven't gotten back from being processed," Prudence said, her glare enough to wither the bravest of souls.

Simon lifted a placating hand. "The four the Taos police have are safe."

"That's not the point. They're ours, and we want them back," my mom said. "We have our ritual to do."

I glanced at Devon. A little while ago, the ladies had disclosed the boxes contained something to do with the sacred Native American ground Luckland was built on. "Do you need the contents to do your ritual?" I asked, a little confused.

The look the ladies gave one another was answer enough, but no one opened their mouth. It didn't seem they would answer Devon's question either.

"So, if anyone contacts you regarding exchanging the cars for the map, please let me know. Immediately. Do I make myself clear?" Devon used his authoritative tone, though it sometimes didn't make a difference.

"I think it's time we head on home." Matilda smiled and took Trey's hand as she stood. "Ladies? Shall we?"

Just like that, they all departed. Even Babs, which left just Dani and Simon. Devon and I shared a glance and a private smile.

"Well, okay. You two know your way around. We'll leave you to it," Devon said, making a point as he took my hand and led me upstairs.

CHAPTER SEVEN

During the next few days, life returned to quasi-normal. I spent time doing inventory at Ye Olde Antique Shoppe, the family business. Dani spent time with her mom, mostly shopping and catching up because they really didn't get to see each other often. Devon and Simon were busy trying to find the cars the old-fashioned way, with police work, because the thief still hadn't contacted anyone regarding exchanging the cars for the map, which worried Devon.

When Friday finally came around, which Devon and I had scheduled for date night, we opted to snuggle and binge-watch our new favorite hoarding show—which lasted all of an hour.

"I'm being summoned," I mumbled into Devon's chest as I read the text on my phone. "The ladies are planning the annual Fourth of July roundup."

"Shouldn't I be summoned as well? They'll need a permit for the fireworks, and they'll have to fill out the proper paperwork."

"We have a town clerk for all that. You don't need to worry."

"Might I remind you that Lois Thorpe *was* the town clerk?"

"Huh. Oh yeah. Guess we need to hire a new one. Or

someone does. You realize we don't have a mayor now that Gus resigned, and his backup was Lois. That leaves only the town council, which as you know…"

"So, the ladies are in charge of themselves? That is not good." Devon shook his head. "When is the next election set for?"

"Whenever the council chooses," I said, then laughed.

"I'm going with you to your mom's. I need to know what's going on in this town. You don't think any of them have political aspirations, do you?"

"You think one of them knocked off Lois so they could become town clerk and thereby acting mayor? That's some theory, Sherlock."

"Actually, I wasn't thinking that, but it is a good theory, Watson."

"According to you, Lois died of natural causes."

Devon grinned. "Got to keep an open mind, Pip. Isn't that what you always say?"

"Nope, *you* always say that. I just remind you."

"Now I'm reminding you that the posse has summoned you, and I'm coming with. Let's mosey off this sofa, shall we?" Devon held his arm around my waist as he sat up to keep me from hitting the floor because sometimes that happened, then he pulled me to my feet. Simon and Dani were off somewhere doing their own thing but had the entry code to get in the house if they got home before we did.

My mom's house appeared awfully dark and quiet when we arrived. All the ladies lived in a row, and from our vantage point, each house seemed empty. Something was off. We rang the bell and waited. I rang it again while Devon checked around the yard then headed down to the sidewalk, looking at the other houses.

"They're gone, aren't they," I called down to him.

"Yeah. Hang on, let me check Prudence's house for the RV." He jogged down to Prudence's, then jogged back without stopping.

"They've taken the RV," he said, coming up the porch steps.

I didn't wait for him to say more. I pulled my phone from my pocket and hit the autodial for my mom. I wasn't sure she'd answer, but I could hope.

"Pip, sorry, we had to reschedule," my mom said even before saying hello.

"Where are you, and where are you headed?"

"We have to go. There's no time to lose."

"What do you mean?" Devon took the phone from my hand.

"We had a phone call. A voice, the same one that threatened us last year, said if we didn't turn over the map, the cars would go the same way as our *friend* Lois."

"When did you get the call? You were supposed to tell me if someone contacted you. Where are you?" Devon demanded.

I could hear my mom sigh. "We've got this. Don't you worry." With that, she hung up. Just great.

Devon looked at me. "I specifically told them to notify me if someone contacted them regarding the cars. I can't believe they ignored me."

"Seriously? I'd be surprised if they didn't ignore you. Those women are a force of their own."

"What are we supposed to do now?"

"I don't suppose you put a tracking device on the RV or one of their phones?" I wouldn't put it past him. He had a tracking app on my phone, so he knew where I was at all times. As an independent woman, I shouldn't have allowed it, but as it comforted him to have the app, I didn't mind.

When Devon shook his head, I sighed. "Okay. We lure them back. I know just the trick."

"Let's hear it."

"What's the one thing those women want, more than finding the gossip-killing car thief?"

"I don't know."

"You do know." I looked at him, trying not to let my nerves show. I hoped he didn't find my brainwave so farfetched he couldn't see what I meant. He looked down at my upturned face, then tucked a stray curl behind my ear, his expression soft.

"Us, together," he whispered, dropping a kiss on my lips while smiling. Still holding my phone, he redialed my mother.

"Pip, I told you—"

"Not Pip, Kate. Devon. You and Matilda need to come home. Pip and I have something to tell you." He smirked, his eyes flashing.

After he disconnected the phone, we looked at each other.

"This is bad, isn't it?" I asked.

"We'll end up paying for it, yeah."

"I wonder who will to be madder, my mom or yours?" I let out a sigh. Tricking them was probably crossing a line, but we couldn't have them going off on a tangent to save the cars on their own. Besides, they didn't have the map—unless they did, and what Devon had was just a copy.

"So, what are we going to tell them?" Devon asked.

"Don't look at me. I already came up with a way to get them back."

"Okay. I got this." He gave me a quick kiss, then escorted me down the steps to the car. We rode home in silence. I wasn't surprised when he let me out of the car and took off, mumbling something about seeing me later. I wasn't sure where he went or what he did, but when he finally came home to bed, either he was incredibly quiet, or I slept like a log.

CHAPTER EIGHT

"THEY LOADED A TRANSPORT TRUCK OFF THE SIDE OF THE ROAD. GKRS." Simon's voice was hushed, but I could hear him clearly from outside the kitchen door. If I entered, however, he and Devon would stop talking.

"Who are they?" Devon asked, his voice low and husky.

"No clue, but my friend at the bureau said their destination is Karson's Kar Shop. Whatever that is." Simon didn't sound too impressed.

"Probably the only mechanic on the island."

What island?

The door suddenly swung open, smacking right into me.

"Oops." Devon chuckled and shook his head. "When are you going to learn, Pippa? Karma's a bitch when you eavesdrop."

"Yeah, yeah, wonder boy. Now, where are the cars headed?" I demanded.

"Don't worry about that. Simon and I have a good lead we're going to follow. You and Dani watch the posse when they return." Devon gave me one of his endearing dimply smiles, knowing I couldn't resist. I should have asked him what I was supposed to say to our mothers when or if they came back. Instead, I nodded.

"Okay, but don't think we won't hunt you down if need be."

"GKRS?" Dani frowned as she searched the internet. "Oh. It's a trucking company."

"Okay, and where is Karson's Kar Shop? It's on an island, apparently."

"Got it covered," Hilda called as she walked into my house uninvited, followed by the rest of the ladies, also uninvited.

"You know which island?" I asked, a little put off. I'd thought Dani and I were the only ones who knew where the cars were headed—other than Devon and Simon.

Prudence waved her arm around. "Of course. We have our own sources."

"What are you all wearing?" Dani stared at them like they'd grown horns.

"Pay no mind, Dani, that's their secret agent outfits." Last time they'd dressed like that was when they broke into my house last year. They were all in black again. This time they wore leggings, leotards, and black ballet slippers. Hilda actually wore it well.

"Okay, ladies, where is the island?" I crossed my arms and waited.

The women all made themselves at home at the card table, my mom emptying a tote bag of drinks and snacks. Unbelievable.

"First, where is Devon, and what do you need to tell us that is so important we had to come back?" My mom gave me the death stare—only it seemed to be tinged with hope. Crap.

"We never said it was important, and I don't know where Devon is. He and Simon went off somewhere. When you didn't come home right away last night, I guess Devon figured you didn't want to hear our news?" I phrased it as a question so as not to lie outright. Otherwise, my face would turn crimson. Couldn't be helped.

"What are you two up to?" Matilda gave me the same look. I knew what they wanted me to say. Devon had hinted our "news" was that we were getting married. They all kept glancing at my hand, frowning when they didn't see a big flashy ring—because that was what they wanted to see.

"When Devon comes back, we'll all have a chat. Now, where is the island? Is that where you were instructed to go?" I asked, standing my ground and refusing to capitulate to their demands.

"Fine. We'll table our talk until later." My mom's voice held *that* tone, the one she used to use when I'd been up to something, like cutting my sister's hair with real scissors when we were five.

Hope cleared her throat. "I think we should explain a few things. First of all, no, the voice didn't mention an island. It told us to head to Vermont, and they'd contact us again the day after tomorrow. However, last night, we found out who picked up the cars. Gus Granville was doing a clean-up on the highway that leads to the cabin and the barn, and a huge semi heading down the mountain at breakneck speed practically ran him off the road. He said he saw the letters GKRS on the side of the truck."

My mom nodded. "It sounded familiar, so I looked it up. They do most of our deliveries at the store. I'm surprised you hadn't realized, Pippa."

She was right. I should have realized as I always met the

delivery truck, but I wanted to know how they found the island. "And?"

"I called them and said one of their trucks might have picked up some antique race cars at our barn and that something was in the cars I needed back. Then I asked them to give me the destination address." My mom looked awfully smug. "I told them I misplaced the sales log."

Hilda cackled. "Well, that young lady didn't even bat an eye, figuratively, of course. She just plain out gave it to us."

"And?" Dani sounded like me now.

"Grand Isle, Vermont, of all places," Prudence announced. "I've been there, you know. Many years ago."

I didn't know that, and I was more than curious, but my curiosity would have to wait. "Did you find out where the cars were headed *before* you got the call demanding the map? Do any of you *have* another map?"

When no one responded, I got my answer. I shook my head. At least I could figure out where Devon and Simon had gone. "Well, what do we do now?"

"If we know *exactly* where the cars are, we can surprise the car thieves instead of being on the back foot. The trucking company hadn't yet delivered the cars, and the young lady told us she'd let us know when they get there. Not much we can do until then. In the meantime, we need to find out how the missing cars are tied to Lois's demise." Matilda looked around the table, then over at us. "Let's get some answers."

She got up from the table, then plonked herself down on the floor. The rest of the ladies followed. I knew what they were up to—some sort of psychic reading or Tarot session. Marcy reached into her bag for her deck. At that point, I was fed up with all the Tarot business. Every time she pulled out that deck, things happened that didn't necessarily have anything to do with the asked questions.

Resigned, Dani and I joined the women. Marcy had told us sitting on the floor brought her closer to her earth elements. Placing her hand over the deck, she tapped it lightly three times, then laid her palm flat on the top.

I assumed she was tapping into Luckland's mystical energy. Over the past year, I'd heard a lot more about the local Native American magic the ladies "used" when they did their annual Founders' Day ritual. According to them, that magical energy also helped increase Marcy's abilities to read Tarot cards and use the Ouija board. Matilda also had some strong intuitive skills, and Hilda's mind reading talent was off the charts, though she'd admitted their skills often didn't work on one of their own. However, Lois wasn't one of their own, so maybe the cards would work this time.

"Lois Thorpe is no longer with us on this earth. The question today, is why?" Marcy asked.

We all waited, staying super quiet while Marcy dealt out some strange pattern of cards on the table. Usually, it was only three to five cards. This time, she dealt more like a dozen. She flipped each one over, then studied it. When she had all the cards she needed face up on the table, she began to scan them. Sometimes, she held her gaze over a card for a minute or more. Other times, she simply slid her gaze over it. Finally, she looked up and sighed.

Hilda broke the silence. "Well?"

"It wasn't Lois's time to die. That is certain." Marcy blew out a breath and shook her head. "Her death is tangled in secrets and lies. Something from the past, her past, is tied to our future. There is danger ahead. But if we remain as one, we will overcome."

I sighed. That was no clearer than any of the other stuff the cards came up with. "Now what?"

"Now we head to the café and figure this out," Matilda

announced as she stood—because in Luckland, if you had a problem to solve, it required nourishment, and pretzels weren't going to cut it.

CHAPTER NINE

THE MOMENT MORGAN CAME OVER TO TAKE OUR ORDERS, I DECIDED TO start a little investigation of my own. Devon hadn't told me if he'd questioned Hunter about the cars, and I wanted to know if Morgan knew anything. "So, Morgan. I haven't seen your boy around lately. Things still cozy with you two?" That sounded innocent enough and shouldn't set off any alarm bells.

"Oh, he, um, had to head out of town... Some conference or another." She didn't look so sure, which surprised me.

"What exactly is he doing these days?" Hope inquired, taking on her librarian tone. "Last I heard, he worked with the construction crew on the Manor before they all quit because they thought the house was haunted."

I loved that Hope pretended not to know what I'd revealed about Hunter and that she'd also gotten in a dig about Hunter and Morgan's involvement with the fiasco last October with their paranormal movie.

Morgan blushed a little at the dig. "Oh, Hunter isn't a construction worker. He was just doing it to help out a friend while in between projects."

"What kind of projects?" Prudence asked. "What is it he does for a living, then?"

"I would have thought you knew." Morgan looked at me, surprised. "Pippa, you didn't tell them!" Morgan smiled. Huh. "Well, he's a research engineer. He mostly gets hired to consult companies looking to discover new mining veins. I'm not really all that up on it, but he uses special maps and tools to find ore. That's how he explained it anyway."

I wasn't sure how accurate she was, but I was quite sure she had no idea what he was really up to. Devon, Simon, and I were positive Hunter was looking for Luckland's gold, and he may well have been the one to steal my dad's cars. I was just about ready to have her sit down with us and maybe talk some sense into her when my phone buzzed, but not with a text.

Devon had access to some pretty super-secret technology, and my phone had a lovely emergency app. So if I were ever in need of immediate assistance, as in my life was in danger, I just tapped the icon on my phone's home screen, and he'd come running. He'd also installed the same app on his phone. However, I never expected him to use it because I doubted he'd call me if his life were in danger.

The emergency icon flashed, and my phone continued to make a weird noise, like the buzzing of a bug zapper, and my heart stopped. Seriously stopped. Everyone stared at me. I took a deep breath and pushed the icon, and a message immediately popped up.

44.7225436 73.2923538

"What is it?" my mother asked, holding a hand up for everyone to be quiet.

"I have no clue. Just numbers," I said, biting my lip nervously.

"Gimme." Dani grabbed the phone. "Hang on," she said as she tapped the numbers into the phone. She looked around the table, making sure everyone was paying attention. "Grand Isle, Vermont. This is the exact latitude and longitude."

Thank god for Dani. I jumped up and grabbed Dani's arm. "Let's go."

Suddenly, Dani's phone buzzed, and she quickly tapped the screen. She turned her phone to me. She had the same message I did.

"You have that on your phone too? Since when? Why didn't you tell me?"

"I didn't know," she whispered.

Wow, she really needed to have a serious talk with Simon.

"What are we waiting for?" Hilda stood. "Let's go. Road trip."

"I'll get the RV," Prudence said.

"It's nearly two thousand miles, Hilda. Prudence, we certainly can't take the RV," I said, somewhat relieved it was that easy to avert disaster. My plan was for Dani and me to fly.

"No, of course not. We'll use it to get to the airport." My mother stood along with the other women, who all began to head for the door. Dani and I froze, looking at each other. My mother turned around. "Well, get a move on if you're coming."

Two hours later, we were in a Lear jet, the kind flown by billionaire executives when they were off for a weekend of golfing and wheeling and dealing. The jet boasted leather sofas and full-size bathrooms, and we had a personal host to take care of our every whim. He was charming too. He announced we'd be flying into Burlington, which was less than a four-hour flight, and said to push the button if we needed anything.

I would have enjoyed myself if I wasn't worried about Devon and Simon. After we'd contacted Grand Isle's police, who had informed us they'd never heard of Karson's Kar Shop and we would need to file a missing person's report before they could go looking for two grown, healthy men who had access to their cell phones, the ladies had decided we would need to rescue Devon and Simon ourselves. I was on board with that.

"Well, what's the plan? Who's got a bright idea? Anyone?"

Hilda lifted her ever-present cane, which only seemed to be a prop, and waved it around. "Listen. I've written enough rescue scenes to know we need a POA, and it better be good. For starters, when we get there, we'll need a war room."

"A what?" Rosa asked

"A place to hunker down in secret. We need to find one of those rent-a-bed places."

"A vacation home?" I glanced at Dani, who already had her phone out. "So, we need a place on the island that sleeps nine." It might be impossible to find something spur of the moment.

"Make sure it has a garage," Matilda said.

"On the water would be nice," Hope remarked.

"Also, a hot tub," Prudence said.

I darted a look at her.

"Really, Pip, we don't know how long we'll be there, and think how romantic it will be when you rescue your boy."

I looked heavenward and sighed.

"Got one," Dani declared. She held out her hand, palm up. The universal sign for *credit card, please.*

As if they'd done their part, everyone went right back to doing their own thing.

"I'm sorry, that's the plan? Rent a place on the lake with a hot tub?"

"And a garage," Hope said as a reminder.

Devon, if you can hear me, hang in there. This may take a while.

CHAPTER TEN

"Pay attention, girls, there are only two ways on and off this island," my mother announced. She, Matilda, Dani, Rosa, and I were in one vehicle, while Prudence, Hope, Marcy, and Hilda were in another. My mom had them on speakerphone.

"This causeway is how we get on and off by road to the mainland. From the other side, a car ferry crosses the lake to New York State."

Hilda's voice came crackling over the speakerphone. "If we rent ourselves a boat, then we'll have a third way off this island."

Dani grinned. "Wow, good thinking, Hilda! I'll get on that in the morning. Boats are my jam anyway."

That was quite true. Dani spent two-thirds of her time on boats as a Master Scuba Diver Instructor and was working on certifying as a Course Director. Training the trainers. If anyone knew boats, it was Dani.

"I wish it weren't so dark," I said quietly, staring out the window at the inky black waterway. "Say, is that our turn up ahead?" I noticed a street sign, and with so few of them, I didn't want to miss our turn.

"No, I'm on it, Pippa," my mom said, reminding me she was the navigator. "Two more up on the right, then down a half mile, and it's on the left."

"Got it," Matilda said. She'd offered to drive as she'd had the largest caffeine fix of anyone on the plane. The combination of espresso and triple chocolate cake would keep her wired up for a good long while.

Pulling into the drive of our vacation hideaway, we all gasped at once. The drive was lined with trees, blocking the street view of the home, which was most definitely waterfront. The circular drive took us underneath an expansive portico, serving as a gateway to an enormous castle in the sand. This was a ridiculous rental.

"Dani, what did you say the fee was on this place?" I asked under my breath, trying not to make a big deal of it.

"I didn't," she whispered back.

Rosa chuckled. "Girls, we can hear you. Out with it, Dani. Quantos?"

Dani smirked. "Two thousand."

"Well, two thousand a week isn't bad," I said.

"Um, no. A night."

Last year, when Devon, Dani, Babs, and I discovered our mothers had found a bag of stolen millions from a Vegas heist thirty years ago, we hadn't understood the extent of their wealth. Investing the millions seemed to have gained them some serious income, which I still couldn't process.

"That's fourteen thousand a week. Over fifty thousand a month. That's..."

"Enough, Pip. Let's get our things inside and figure out something for dinner." My mother's tone had a bite to it. I must have stepped over a line. Who could blame me? I'd spent the last decade struggling to build a career as an outdoor photographer and blogger, enough to make a living, only to discover I didn't need to. However, I didn't really believe that. Nobody should be lazy in life. Still, they could have told us years ago we had more than enough money to help us through the difficult times.

The house was stunning, sparkling clean, and ready for guests. Everything had a wonderful New England seaside motif as if we were in a seaside cottage rather than a castle. The massive kitchen overlooked the lake. Sadly, as with most vacation homes, the stunning five-door refrigerator was empty save a case of water bottles and a box of baking soda. The cupboards were also bare.

"How much are you all willing to pay for a pizza?" Dani asked, phone to her ear.

"Depends," said Hilda. "Real pizza or one of those chains."

Dani listened for a moment, then grinned. "He says it's as real as it gets. His grandfather was a third Italian. He can have a few pies here in about an hour."

"Opening bid?" I asked, a bit cheekily.

"Easy. Fifty dollars for the pies and a hundred for the delivery," Hope answered, loud enough for our pizza guy to hear.

Dani nodded and looked up. "Cash?"

Prudence pulled a wad of bills out of her purse and flipped through it.

"Done," she said with a nod.

Well, one problem down. I really needed to find Devon. Knowing he was in danger physically hurt. I tried to stay encouraged, assuming Hunter, or whoever had them, wouldn't hurt them. I looked at Dani, who stared out the kitchen window. I knew she hoped the same thing.

I moved to stand beside her. "We'll find them, Dani. Don't doubt that for a moment." I spoke softly but with determination, my focus on the darkness as I sent a mental message to the powers that be.

"First thing in the morning, we'll go into town and hit the marina. Find ourselves a boat. I'm sure they've got some nice rentals," Dani said. "Something with a little meat on its bones."

"Translation?" I knew next to nothing about boats.

"Speed and power. Once we find Devon and Simon, we'll need to power it up and get the hell out at breakneck speed."

"Do we though? Once we release them from Hunter's clutches, wouldn't Devon and Simon arrest him and whoever he's working with?"

"What if they get away and use a boat to do so? At least we'd have something ready to give chase if that happened."

I conceded Dani's point. "Okay. I'll leave everything regarding the boat to you."

When our pizza arrived, the lucky delivery guy grinned like a fool as he pulled out a few bottles of wine to surprise us, which earned him more than a few hugs and kisses from the posse and wiped that grin right off his young, handsome face.

Settling in on the massive deck out back, we ate and drank in silence. Each of us lost in our own thoughts about what the next day might bring.

CHAPTER ELEVEN

"Dani, tell me that isn't what I think it is?" I whispered, afraid to know the answer as Dani and I looked out the large window over the kitchen sink as bright sunshine lit up the early morning and sparkled off the water.

"Are you thinking it's a ridiculously ostentatious yacht for cruising in the Caribbean rather than a fast, pursuit boat?"

"Pretty much."

"You know who's missing right now?"

I looked about the kitchen and sighed. "Hilda."

"Marcy, your aunt has lost her mind, hasn't she?" Dani asked.

Prudence snorted. "Newsflash, that train has left the station."

"That boat is going to get all kinds of unwanted attention. We don't want anyone knowing we're here on the island until we find the boys," Hope declared, shaking her head.

"Might as well make the most of it," Matilda said.

What?

The women looked at one another with a gleam in their eyes. This mission was destined for doom.

As the boat pulled next to the oversized dock, with an actual *boathouse* attached, the women quickly hustled out of the kitchen, leaving Dani and me to ponder what would happen next.

"You don't think she'll crash that thing, do you?"

"She's not piloting that beast. I don't think," Dani said.

"Thanks for the reassurance," I muttered. "Now what?"

"Let's go out there and see what she's brought us." Dani headed for the patio doors and slid them open to the luxurious deck. The stairs led to a boardwalk, which in turn led to the dock. Hilda stood proudly at the rail at the front of the boat. Someone else tied the boat to the dock, which thankfully meant Hilda hadn't been the one steering the damn thing.

"Ahoy, mateys," she called out with a laugh. "I found us a boat!"

"Hilda," I said as Dani and I strode over to join her on the deck. "I'm fairly certain we mentioned the boat should be discreet."

Hilda snickered. "Have you never heard of hiding in plain sight?"

"Hilda, this isn't plain sight. It's more like Captain Obvious," I said with as much patience as I could manage.

We turned as an older gentleman dressed in a captain's uniform approached.

"Girls, this is Captain Olaf Van De Guard. He's graciously agreed to be on call for us. His boat was over at the marina, which is quite full of riffraff this time of year, and I offered private docking here in exchange for a ride if needed."

"Ladies." The captain bowed. He was the quintessential seaman—snowy white hair, a neatly trimmed beard, and a ruddy complexion, which I hadn't expected. I would have thought whoever captained this boat would be more of the suave, debonaire type.

"Yoo-hoo!"

My stomach sank. That singsong tone in Matilda's voice was never a good omen.

"Hello, there!" my mother called.

"Oh, what a lovely idea! A boat ride!" Hope declared.

Dani and I stared in horror as they got closer. Gone were the robes and slippers they'd worn in the kitchen earlier. They had dressed for some serious yachting—striped boatneck cotton tops in various shades of blue with red and white linen capris, docksiders, big floppy straw hats, sunglasses, and tote bags. I wouldn't have been surprised to find out they had all that packed in the Luxmobile for just such an occasion. The women were nothing if not prepared for any eventuality. Of course, they were already en route to the island before coming back to find me at the Manor, so they'd at least planned on being here.

After they'd all boarded, Dani and I quickly hopped back onto the dock. We watched the boat glide away, the women all standing and waving at us. Upon closer examination, they weren't waving at all; they were toasting one another.

My phone buzzed. Incoming text. I tapped the screen to see the message.

Devon: Babe, lost my keys, leave back door open.

I looked at Dani, my eyes wide. Turning my phone so she could read the screen, I waited for her reaction.

"He's back in Luckland?" Dani asked.

I shook my head almost violently.

"Spit it out, Pip. What is it?"

I took a breath. "That's not Devon. Or he's using code."

"Are you sure?"

"Totally. If Devon sent that, he most certainly doesn't mean a word of it."

Another buzz.

Devon: Why don't you grill those two steaks in the frzr 2night?"

I sat down on the nearest lounge chair and pondered what the hell he was saying.

"Okay, Pip, let's analyze this," Dani said. "He knows we're not in Luckland. He'd have known we'd leave once we realized he was in trouble."

"Right. He also knows calling me babe means no sex for a very long time." I looked up at Dani as she laughed out loud. I smiled. "We don't have keys. We have an app-controlled keypad."

"And you, my friend, do not grill." Dani smirked as she said that last bit.

"No, but I think I know what he means. Two steaks, two people. So, they're being held by two people. Tonight means to come after dark. Only we don't know exactly where they are yet. We need to know the exact location of the delivery."

Dani's phone buzzed just then.

"What? Who is it?" I asked.

"Simon. He says he's found the perfect spot for our bike ride."

"Bike ride?"

"I assume he's telling us not to use cars to search the island because whoever is holding them hostage will hear the vehicle's engine if we get too close to the building."

"That kind of makes sense. So, what now?"

"Let's get those seafaring women back here, stat."

"Stat?"

"It's what I tell my divers. If I say right now, they take it as an invitation to dillydally."

"Dillydally?"

"Yes, oh little parrot. Dillydally. Come on. We've got plans to make." Dani was suddenly in take-charge mode. The

instructor in her, I guessed. A woman training Navy SEALs had to have a pretty stiff backbone.

I sent off a group text to the ladies.

Me: Back to the lake house now! Emergency!

Thirty seconds later, I got a reply.

Mom: Roger that.

I shook my head and prayed Dani knew how to use the coffeemaker in the kitchen. I was going to need at least another double shot of caffeine for this. First though, I needed to reassure my guy he was in good hands.

Me: Out of propane. I'll see what Lali's got for me.

"Let me see what you wrote," Dani leaned over to look at my screen, then eyed me curiously.

"We have a gas grill, not propane. And I hope to god he remembers Lali is the ladies' psychic in Sedona."

"How will all that help?" asked Dani.

"My mentioning propane tells him I know it's all a ruse. My mentioning Lali means I'll try to get some answers to find him. At least that's what I'm trying to say. Maybe they're not paying any attention to his phone at all, but I doubt it."

CHAPTER TWELVE

JUST AS THE WOMEN RETURNED TO SHORE, MY MOM'S PHONE RANG. Everyone stopped what they were doing as Mom listened. When she hung up, she turned to us.

"Well, we're definitely in the right place. The voice said to make our way to Grand Isle and wait for more instructions tonight."

"That's it?" I asked. "Nothing more?"

My mom shook her head. "No."

"So, we've lost our element of surprise," Dani said.

"Not necessarily. They don't know we're already here. We still have time to find Karson's Kar Shop and form a plan of attack," I said.

The women agreed, and Dani and I spent the next few minutes explaining the texts we'd received and why we needed to search on foot, or in our case, on bicycles.

"Oh, I do love a good hog," Hilda said.

Hog?

"No, Hilda, bicycles, not motorcycles." Dani shook her head and grinned.

"No. You all can do the whole bicycle thing. I'll get myself a

Harley, thank you." Hilda was quite adamant. Not an ounce of humor in her voice.

My mom sighed. "Look, we'll discuss it when we get to town. First, we need a bike store."

"Already on it, Mom," I said. "Earl's Cyclery. I don't know if they rent though."

"Rent, buy, whatever. We need bikes, so we get bikes," Matilda announced.

"All right, we'll... Oh shit, never mind. Closed on Sundays."

"Puhlease," Matilda said. "Who owns the place? Call them."

I gnawed on my lower lip. I wasn't as brazen as the others. I was a bit of a people pleaser in that regard. Though weighing my options, I didn't have a choice. Devon needed me. I had to suck it up. It didn't take long to find a number for the owners, but I made sure the phone wasn't on speaker because this guy would probably hang up in a heartbeat if these women started talking all at the same time as they were wont to do.

The phone rang for quite a long while, and I had almost hung up when someone finally answered.

"Talk to me." The voice sounded impatient. I was probably interrupting a good Sunday sleep in.

"Yeah, um, I'm calling about the cycle shop."

"We're closed."

"Yes, I understand, being Sunday and all, but we need to get a few bikes, and we kind of need them today."

"A few? How many is a few?"

"Nine."

"What kind of bikes are we talking about?"

"Not sure? Sturdy, dependable, easy to ride, for women?"

"You want nine women's bikes. Now. What's the budget for this?"

I had no idea how much a new bike was. I hadn't bought one in a while. I glanced at Dani and mouthed *how much?*

She held up one finger.

A hundred?

She shook her head.

A thousand?

She nodded.

"Can we keep it under a thousand each?" I knew it was silly to bargain when they weren't even open. "Unless, of course, we can just rent them."

"No rentals. Okay. Meet me in fifteen minutes at the shop. Not sure I have nine available, but we'll see what we have."

I thanked him profusely and hung up.

"Quick, everyone in the cars, we've got fifteen minutes to find this place."

<hr>

"No. I will not get on that." Hilda glared at the beautiful bike we'd chosen for her. It was a gorgeous dusty rose with a wide cushioned seat and a nifty electric power assist. I didn't under-stand her reluctance because it was perfect for her.

"As a matter-of-fact, I think I should go home. To Luckland. When you're through here, you can just drop me at the airport."

I frowned. "What? Why?" Then I saw the fear in her eyes. I gently took her arm and escorted her off to the side. "You can't ride, can you?" I asked softly. She shook her head.

"But, Pippa, that stays between us. I really do want to go to Luckland. I think someone there is going to get into mischief while we're gone. And none of us are there to look out for it." She spoke quietly but firmly.

"My dad, Trey, and Martin are all there. We could have them keep a lookout."

Hilda's expression turned priceless. She tipped her head

sideways and rolled her eyes. "Girl, those boys have hearts of gold, but they're not cut out for this."

"Martin is a deputy, Hilda. Of course, he is."

"Look, if we all get into trouble here, they'll have to come and bail us out. We need someone there to stay put and mind the store. That's me. I may be spry and my mind sharp as a tack, but I could slow you all down. You need to focus on saving your man."

I sighed, but she was right. If we left her alone, at the house or the boat, we'd worry about her. "Okay. I'll back you up on this."

"Thanks. Let me do the talking, got it?" Considering Hilda's storytelling capacity, I was certainly happy to let her spin her own tale.

CHAPTER THIRTEEN

"WE'LL RIDE IN PAIRS, DON'T WANT ANYONE GETTING LOST, HURT OR god forbid, kidnapped." Suddenly, my mom became leader of the pack—a woman who hadn't ridden a bike in years. Most of them could ride though. I'd seen old photos of them posing with their bicycles. No helmets, of course. Back then, they weren't a thing, but times had changed, and with their highly unique choices in helmets, also courtesy of the bike shop, they were quite the crew.

"You all look ready for the Tour de France!" I said.

Hardly. More like the Tour de Luckland. They were back in their black leggings, this time with matching Earl's t-shirts—a gift the bike shop owner threw in because he'd just sold eight bikes, all with the electric power assist. He'd discounted them, having no idea these women could have bought the entire store, but he was happy, and so were they. He even offered to ship them to Luckland when they were through with their "bike tour." Had he known their true mission, I wondered if he would have kicked in a few extras. Or kicked them out.

It was already late afternoon by the time Marcy and Hope had returned from driving Hilda to the airport, and the rest of us had hauled the bikes to the house, which took several trips. Then we decided we all needed some practice, so we went up and down the driveway of the *Luckland Ladies Lakefront Lodge,* so named by Hope. They'd already decided to make an offer on the place—once we'd rescued our boys, of course.

After we all managed to correct wobbles and stay upright, we mapped out our plan. Without Hilda, we were an even eight. So, we divided ourselves into four teams.

"Okay, I need one team to ride north up W Shore Rd. This is us right here." Dani pointed and drew a circle on the map where the house was. "Kate, you and Tillie go that way. Hope, you and Marcy head south. Pru and Mama, you head east on Allen, and Pip and I will take this over to Pearl. Everyone got their maps on their phones and ready to go?"

Prudence grinned. "Ready as we'll ever be! Oh, look, Rosa, that will take us to Route 2, which takes us to that wonderful little snack bar. Who wants clams? We'll bring some back."

"How do you know they have clams?" I asked.

"I've been here before, remember," Pru replied, her tone smug.

"Well, can we please find Devon and Simon first?" I couldn't help my scathing tone. Seriously, didn't these women realize the importance of our mission?

"Of course, dear, but we do have to eat. Keep up our strength and all," Rosa said, ever the mediator and the voice of reason.

"All right, ladies, let's go." My mother pointed down the driveway. We all hopped on our bikes and began what I hoped would be a fruitful search for our missing guys.

"There. Look," I whispered as I pointed at a thick outcrop of pine trees along the bend in the road. I'd noticed an old gravel drive with fresh tire tracks. So as not to be obvious, we rode a little farther up the road and stopped.

We'd already looked for Karson's Kar Shop's address online, but it hadn't shown up, meaning it had to be an underground business of some sort—which I'd recently seen on an episode of one of those true crime shows. So then, via satellite maps, we searched properties with hangars, barns, or really large workshops.

After a while, it became apparent that trying to electronically find a suitable building that could house the two missing cars was impossible. Devon and Simon must have known, which was why they'd mentioned the bikes. Of course, they hadn't known the posse was with us.

"Take a panoramic picture, Pip, and turn on the location markings."

I did as Dani suggested. Then I loaded my GPS map on my phone and looked at the satellite imagery. The drive led to a clearing, and in that clearing were several building structures. Outside those buildings, at least on the particular day the satellite caught the image, cars littered the property. I couldn't zoom in all the way, but enough to see they weren't ordinary passenger vehicles—more like stock cars with junk parts laying around. I dropped a location pin, then googled the address.

WR Karson. Looked like we'd found Karson's Kar Shop, which, I hoped, meant we'd found Devon and Simon.

***

Lakefront Lodge's living room had become our proverbial war room. Instead of sitting around a long conference table, however, we'd scattered on exceptionally comfortable sofas and recliners with an exquisite view of the lake.

"Now we have Devon and Simon's location, why don't we just call the cops again?" I asked.

My mom shook her head. "I think it's best we handle this discreetly. No telling the fallout if someone leaked that somebody held Luckland's finest and an FBI agent hostage." Her phone buzzed, and she glanced at the screen. "Well, that isn't going to help."

"What?" I demanded. "What won't help?"

"Your father and Trey are headed here."

Prudence nodded as she waved her phone. "Marty says they couldn't be talked out of it, and they left this morning." She sighed. "I wish he'd have come as well. But you know someone has to mind the town."

Dani smirked. "I thought that was Hilda's job. She should be back there any time now."

"Ladies, ladies," Hope said. "No time for this. We've got to get those boys. Dani, did you send Simon a text, telling him you were looking forward to the bike ride?"

"Affirmative, Hope."

"Pippa, what did you send Devon?"

"I texted him that Lali found some propane, and I looked forward to grilling the steaks."

Prudence smiled at me. "Oh, very good, Pip. Well done."

"I thought so."

My mom's phone rang, and she frowned as she answered it. A few seconds later, she put it on speaker. *"Or we'll sink the cars. With your most valuable cargo aboard."*

The call disconnected as everyone stared. The voice had sounded muffled, as if someone had spoken through a cloth or something.

"Is that..."

My mom nodded. "They said they want the map. You heard the rest."

"Over my dead body," I yelled. "Let's go. We're going there now. Enough of this."

"No, Pippa. This is our fight, not yours," my mother said quietly, meaning Hope, Prudence, Matilda, and herself.

"No, Kate. This fight belongs to all of us," my father said as he and Trey stormed through the front door. I couldn't say I wasn't overjoyed to see them. Well, my dad, at least. I needed his reassurance. He was my dad, after all. He could save the universe.

As my mom gazed up at him and smiled softly, I realized their bond went far deeper than I'd previously understood. There was some secret tacit understanding between them that had escaped me until that moment. He'd come to Vermont because she was here, and he needed to be with her to face her battles—just as I'd come to Vermont to do the same for Devon.

CHAPTER FOURTEEN

"As soon as they tell me where to bring the map, Matilda and I will head out." My mom stood on the deck by the rail overlooking the shore. My dad stood next to her, his arm about her shoulders.

"I'm going with you," he said quietly, but not so quietly I didn't hear him.

She shook her head just as her phone rang. Everyone tensed, especially my father. Mom answered her phone and put it on speaker.

"Come to the intersection of Allen and Shore. You have twenty minutes."

When the call ended, she looked at me. "That's where you said you found the car yard, Pippa." My mom straightened her shoulders, then nodded once. "I'm ready."

"The map? Do you have a copy?" I asked. None of them had answered the last time I'd asked, but I hoped they'd answer this time.

"We have a copy of something else, something similar." She sounded smug with not a shred of nervousness.

She headed into the house, then out the front door,

Matilda right beside her. I started to follow. No way was I letting them go on their own. Seemed my dad and Trey had the same idea because they beelined it after them. I shot a quick text to Babs, who was probably chewing off all her nails.

Me: This is it. If you don't hear from me in an hour, call out the troops. Location is Shore and Allen. Grand Isle, VT.

I also sent her the location pin.

We all must have looked ridiculous—my mother and Matilda marching up the road, followed about a hundred yards or so by my dad and Trey, then by Dani and me. The moon shone brightly, affording us enough light to get by without flashlights, though I jumped at every shadow that moved.

My mom neared the intersection, then, without warning, she disappeared. We all ran to Matilda, where she stood alone.

"Tillie, what the hell just happened?" my dad demanded.

"A woman. With a gun. Tailored suit, snow-white hair, and a string of pearls around her neck."

I knew instantly who that was, which must have been evident by my expression.

My dad grabbed my arm. "What? What is it, Pip?"

"I know who it is." I took a deep breath to dampen my shock. "We need to follow them. Right now. No time to waste," I muttered as I headed up the gravel drive Dani and I had found earlier. If that woman thought she would destroy my family, she had another think coming.

As we approached the same clearing I'd seen on the satellite photo, several buildings appeared. Most of the buildings were dark, but a sliver of light streamed from a small window on a low square building toward the back of the property. We clung to the tree line surrounding the clearing, trying to remain out of sight.

The building turned out to be some sort of garage with three large metal doors, between which were several high windows. My dad clamped his hand on my shoulder.

"Where there's a garage, there's a ladder. Trust me." He patted me for luck, looked about, then crouched and approached the building. The rest of us stood still as church mice and watched. Then he disappeared around the side of the building. Several agonizing minutes went by before he reappeared carrying something odd.

As he got closer, I shook my head. "Dad," I whispered. "That's not a ladder."

"No, but it'll do the trick." He smiled like the childhood neighborhood pogo champ he'd been.

"You aren't seriously going to use that?" I asked.

"We need to see inside, which means we need height. This will do it."

"Dad, no offense, but you're not twelve anymore."

"It's like riding a bike, Pip. As you well know, you never forget."

I didn't really know what to do at that point. My dad headed over to a spot just below one of the windows, then started bouncing off the ground on a pogo stick. Higher and higher and higher until he could see inside the little window. Each bounce lasted only seconds. He had to bounce a few times to get a good look. Finally, he stopped. I sighed with relief. Not just because he hadn't broken a leg or worse, but the pogo stick wasn't the quietest—every bounce made a little squeak, but hopefully not loud enough for anyone inside to hear.

He huddled up to us, pogo stick still in hand. "Your mother is safe. She's in a chair at a table. Looks like her arms are behind her back. Devon and Simon are behind her, against the wall, on the floor. It seems like their hands are also behind their backs. Hunter is at the table with your mother. She looks pissed off, by the way."

That made me smile. My mother, when angry, was a firecracker. She hardly ever displayed her anger, so when she did, it was an event.

"The lady in the suit is standing to the side, holding a gun and waving it back and forth between your mom and the boys. She looks pissed off too."

"Only two of them?" I wasn't surprised to find out Hunter was there—we'd all figured he must have been part of the car theft.

"Yes. We can take them, I'm sure. You, Dani, and Tillie have some serious self-defense training. Trey and I can distract the woman."

"And how do you figure that?" I asked.

"I've got a black belt. I suggest you let me take the lead," Trey stated.

"Oh my god, you seriously do?" I spoke before thinking. Matilda had told us Trey had a black belt when it seemed he'd killed a man. Thankfully, Trey had only hit him in self-defense.

"Of course. Didn't Tillie mention it?" He looked at Matilda and smiled.

"She did, but we kind of thought it was just a pickup line. Sorry."

Trey grinned. "No worries. So, first rule, we need to be prepared. We don't just go charging in."

My dad nodded. "Agreed."

"Wait. Considering they have a gun, I think we need to call in a favor, and I know just who to call." With that, Dani fired off a text, held her hand up to indicate we should wait a moment, then smiled. "Help is on the way. ETA about an hour."

We all turned suddenly at the crunch of gravel. Prudence,

Hope, Marcy, and Rosa came down the drive. Rosa carried a ladder.

While Trey and my dad ran over to take the ladder, I turned to Dani. "This is your help?"

Dani shook her head. "Not in this lifetime. Nothing but coincidence."

"I called for reinforcements," Matilda said.

I couldn't complain. I wanted to see what was going on, and as pogo sticks weren't my forte, I needed a ladder.

I went along with my dad and Trey as they quietly made their way over to the building and leaned the ladder against it. Before either could climb it, I had my foot on the bottom rung, causing my dad to scowl.

"I need this, Dad," I whispered as I began to climb.

CHAPTER FIFTEEN

PEERING THROUGH THE WINDOW, I ALMOST FELL OFF THE LADDER. I certainly wobbled. Belle Chantelle waved her arms about and yelled something. She held a large piece of paper in one hand, which I assumed was the "map" my mom had with her. As my dad had described, Simon and Devon sat on the floor while Hunter sat at the table with my mom. I couldn't hear what Belle was saying but realized the window wasn't latched shut, so I gently grabbed onto the bottom frame and tugged. It didn't move far, but enough for me to hear.

"Who are the four winds? What is that? It's you. I know it."

Four winds?

"It says here when the four winds gather, entrance shall be granted." Belle waited. So did I. I'd never heard of the four winds. My mother just shrugged, her expression blank. I knew that look. It was a trick she'd shown Babs and me. When we were younger, she taught us that if someone tried to bully us, we should travel somewhere pleasant in our minds, tune out whatever was being said, and blank our facial expressions, which was exactly what she was doing. *Well done, Mom.*

The ladder vibrated, and I looked down.

"Time for the main act. Climb down," Dani whispered.

After I reached the bottom, Dani grabbed my hand, and we headed back to the others.

"Any change?" Dad asked.

"No, but as I suspected, white hair lady is Belle Chantelle. She's got the map Mom brought and is ranting about four winds."

"Belle Chantelle? That's who's in there?" Matilda asked, hands on hips.

"The very one."

"I should have known," Prudence remarked. "She was never one of us. She was a wannabe."

"Okay, sorry, but who is Belle Chantelle?" Trey asked.

"Trey, I'd love to explain, but we just don't have the time at the moment, but I promise, once we have the boys and my mom safe, we'll all have a nice long chat." I was nervous and hyped up. I just wanted this over with. "Dani? You said it was time for the main act?"

"Yes. Any minute now, my SEALs friends stationed near here will fly a chopper above us and shine a searchlight over the property. This should draw our car thieves out of the building. Trey, you and Colin try and round them up, and Pippa and I will go in and get Kate and the boys."

"What if Hunter has a gun too? I couldn't see one, but we can't discount it," I said.

"Don't you worry, Pip. Trey and I can handle them." My dad sounded confident, and I trusted him.

The promised chopper approached, and within seconds the brightest searchlight I'd ever seen traced a swath over the building. A door flew open on the side of the building, and two figures came out, stopping short when the light passed over them. My dad and Trey ran at them like charging bears. I barely had time to think before Dani grabbed my hand, and we sprinted into the building, the posse right behind us. They headed straight over to the table where my mom sat while Dani and I dashed to the wall where the boys were already trying to loosen the rope that bound their wrists.

I reached behind Devon, who had the silliest grin as he turned his head to watch what I was doing. The moment I finished untying the rope, he grabbed me around the waist and pulled me onto his lap. Then without warning, he kissed me senseless, stealing my breath away.

"What was that for?" I smiled and put a finger to his lips.

"For figuring it out." Mimicking my actions, he put one of his fingers on my lips and gazed at me. We were having a moment—which Simon, who was on his feet by then, completely ruined by producing a fake cough and smirking at us.

I would have said something about the way he rested his hand on Dani's arm, but just then, my dad and Trey rushed in, huffing and wheezing.

"We lost 'em!" my dad said between breaths.

"We tried," Trey said. "Too many trees."

"Then we're not safe," Simon said, oddly quite relaxed and matter-of-fact for someone who'd been held hostage by gun-toting, car-thieving gold diggers.

My dad, who had his arms protectively around my mom, looked around the room and realized what was in there. "My babies," he whispered, gazing at his Alfettas.

Devon nodded. "They arrived about an hour ago."

I assumed that prompted Belle to call and demand my mom bring the map. I still didn't understand why Belle thought the ladies would hand over a map worth probable millions for cars a fraction of that value. Devon and Simon's value, however... Priceless.

"Colin, we'll take care of those tomorrow," my mom said, her voice laced with humor.

"Sorry, love." He gave her a squeeze and kissed her forehead. I smiled because they rarely showed any PDA, and I wished they'd show more.

Hope suddenly clapped her hands. "Let's go, troops. We need to regroup, and we can't hang out here all night. We'll head back to Lakefront Lodge and figure out what's next."

She took Marcy's hand, then headed out the open door with everyone right behind them. Devon shifted me off his lap so he could stand and pull me up.

"You had me worried, Kemosabe,' I whispered once we were outside and a good distance behind everyone else.

Devon smiled. "You were worried? About me?"

I nodded. "It wasn't a nice emotion."

"You certainly proved yourself, Pip. You found us."

"This time. I'm not sure I'm cut out for this kind of search and rescue though."

"Don't sell yourself short. We make a good team, you and I."

I looked up at him. He wasn't talking about investigating.

CHAPTER SIXTEEN

As we approached the drive to the house, Devon stopped and tugged my hand, indicating I should also stop.

"Pippa. This is the house you rented?"

"Wasn't me. Dani found it."

"You realize most recognizance missions are done discreetly, right?"

"Are you implying Lakefront Lodge is not the epitome of discretion?"

He chuckled. "I am. Next time, perhaps you ought to lean more toward a cozy cottage."

"You haven't seen the inside." I grinned. He was going to flip at the gourmet kitchen.

I was right about Devon's reaction to the house. Giving him a tour was fun. It would have been more fun had my phone not buzzed as we stood at the upstairs window that overlooked the lake, his palm on my cheek as he gazed into my eyes.

Mom: Emergency, the dock.

I groaned, then turned to race down the stairs.

"What's going on?" Devon asked as he ran after me.

"Emergency at the dock."

Devon and I headed outside, where everyone had gathered around something or, as it turned out, someone.

Captain Olaf. "Wait, the boat's gone, and Olaf's here?"

"Who and what are you talking about, Pip?"

I stopped and turned to Devon. "Long story short, Hilda rented us a yacht in case we needed to chase the car thieves across the lake. Dani suggested something faster, but the yacht was what Hilda came up with. Olaf owned and captained the yacht."

"What kind of yacht, and where is Hilda?"

"Afraid of bikes, so she went home. A very, very expensive yacht."

Devon nodded and stared across the dark water. "Ironically, I'm guessing it's become a getaway vehicle. Let's find out."

The ladies stepped back to let Devon through. Simon was already crouched next to Olaf, who looked a little dazed.

"What do we have?" Devon asked.

"Devon, this is Captain Van De Guard. Seems a pair of thieves took off with his boat," Simon replied.

"Had guns, they did." Olaf shrugged. He really did not seem seriously distressed, which Devon seemed to have spotted right away.

"Captain Van De Guard, forgive me, but you don't seem too concerned about the boat. I take it it's insured?"

"Well, I wouldn't know about that."

"You wouldn't?" I spoke before thinking, causing Devon and Simon to shoot me a look.

"How about a license to pilot it?" Simon asked.

"Eh, nope, afraid not."

"Might I inquire, sir, who owns the boat?" Devon was being very polite.

"Well." Olaf took off his cap and scratched his head. "I don't rightly know. I just park 'em."

Simon and Devon kept their expressions neutral and nodded. The rest of us had our mouths open.

I regrouped and said the first thing that came to mind. "You're a valet parking attendant for yachts?" I looked at Dani, the only one with actual boat knowledge, particularly about marinas. She shook her head, holding in a laugh.

"Close enough, Pip. We'll chat later." I figured I had that coming. I knew next to nothing about boats. Or boathouses, for that matter.

Once Devon and Simon had taken care of reporting the stolen boat, which I was sure they did discreetly, and my dad had offered Olaf a ride back to the marina, we finally opened the door to the boathouse.

It turned out to be a large bunkhouse that probably could have slept ten with a little maneuvering. One side had a sitting area, the other a sleeping area with four adult-sized bunk beds. In the center sat a full gourmet kitchen. I grinned at the electronic sign on the back wall hanging over a doorway that flashed "Restroom" in green, which I imagined was for the benefit of boaters who'd been waiting to relieve themselves for hours.

I could see myself on a summer's day, lounging in the comfy sitting area with its wall-to-wall and floor-to-ceiling windows, perfect for reading in or photographing the lake.

"Devon, I could literally live here year-round. Just in this boathouse. Hope said my mom had it in her head to buy the property."

Devon grinned. "You're probably already cranking those wheels in your head to help seal the deal. Though you're not seriously considering moving here, are you?" He suddenly frowned.

"No, not ever. But a vacation home would be lovely, don't ya think?" I grinned back.

"Hey, Devon, I think we should bunk out here," Simon called from the other side of the room. "We don't want all of us to be in one place if they return."

"Good call. We can keep watch out here." Devon headed over to formulate a plan.

As the ladies headed inside the house, Dani and I stepped onto the dock to enjoy the nighttime breeze coming off the lake. Rosa stopped beside us.

"Is anything wrong?" Dani asked her mother.

"Not at all. I noticed you and Simon having a little time together on the walk back. Just wondering, is all." Rosa grinned, making me chuckle.

"Exactly, Dani. What's going on between you? It's time to fess up."

"Why does everyone think there's something between Simon and me? I've told you both. Nothing to see. Move along." Dani thinned her lips in frustration. I knew that look well, and it was best to stop needling her, or she'd start in on me. She must have been more than frustrated, however, because she narrowed her eyes as she turned in my direction.

"What about you and Devon? How would you like it if I kept asking why he hasn't put a ring on it?"

I didn't really know how to answer that. Devon and I had been a couple for a year, but we were exclusive, and we'd moved in together. It was enough. However, we'd known each other our whole lives, and everyone and their mothers were waiting for something more permanent to happen, and they were getting impatient.

Just as I was formulating a response, Devon stepped outside.

"Am I interrupting?" His gaze flicked from Dani to Rosa to me.

"Nope. We're all good out here. Just getting ready to head up to the house."

"I'll walk you," he said abruptly, taking my hand.

Damn it. I was sure he'd heard more than he should have. It had happened before. I tended to blurt out things before ensuring it was safe to do so. I just hoped he didn't go telling Simon what Dani had said.

CHAPTER SEVENTEEN

"The coast guard located the yacht," Devon said as he came strolling into the kitchen as if he owned the place, followed by Simon, my dad, and Trey. They all had travel-size mugs of coffee and looked refreshed. The boathouse must have been quite comfortable.

"And Belle?" I immediately asked from my perch at the peninsula. Dani and I had been the first downstairs, as the women weren't known to rise early.

"How about we get everyone down here, so we don't have to do this twice." Simon chuckled. He knew the routine—anyone who wasn't present for an update would demand to hear it all over again.

"Then one of you will have to wake them all 'cause I'm not doing it." Dani was still in a bit of a snit after last night's conversation.

Thankfully, my dad volunteered, and within fifteen minutes, everyone invaded the kitchen and grabbed a seat. Devon and Simon chose to stand. They leaned against the counter by the window overlooking the lake, their postures identical—one arm across the chest, hand grasping their side, the other hand holding a mug.

"Ready when you are, Devon," Matilda said, nodding from her imperial perch at the end of the long counter.

"Simon?" Devon turned to Simon and tipped his head. They had a silent conversation, then Simon placed his mug down and stepped forward.

"The yacht was found moored up north toward the Canadian border, a little public boat access called Sandy Point. No sign of anyone on board. I can't share the owner's name just yet. We're still verifying it, and we have to rule out their involvement."

"Do you think Olaf was telling the truth?" Hope asked.

"We'll let you know when we know," Devon answered, which earned a glare from Hope.

"What now?" my mom asked. "Back to Luckland, or do we wait until they're caught?"

"Back to Luckland, Kate," Devon said. "There are a few flights a day out of Burlington, so we should all be able to get back tonight."

"Devon, we'll take care of the arrangements." Matilda's voice held a warning. "We got ourselves here, and we can get us all home."

"What does that even mean, Mom?" Devon frowned. He was a take-charge kind of guy, much like his mother, and when the two butted heads, it usually ended in a standoff.

"Give me a few minutes, and I'll have it all arranged. As you like to say, it's a need-to-know kind of thing."

"That's only for a criminal investigation, not plane tickets," he grumbled.

I darted a look at him, one that implied it was all fine and to relax. He frowned at me but nodded.

He was still grumpy as we all boarded the Lear jet for the return home. My dad and Trey, however, rented a special trailer and were driving back with the Alfettas. We wouldn't see either of them for a week, most likely. My dad and Trey were becoming quite good friends, which I thought was good for both of them, though I sensed the ladies worried the men would soon have their own posse—and that would never do.

The ladies were quite talkative on the plane. From the bits and pieces I overheard, they seemed to be making plans to try and give my mom her grand opening event at the Playhouse once again. I was never sure how they went from crime victims in the throes of a potential murder investigation to party planners without blinking an eye, though they made it appear seamless and natural.

We were a few hours into the flight when Devon leaned toward me. "Penny for your thoughts," he said quietly.

I'd been wondering how Lois Thorpe and Belle Chantelle were connected, what the connection was between Hunter and Belle, and whether Morgan was involved with Lois's death or the car theft. "A penny is not nearly enough," I replied with a smile. "I'll take a dollar."

He smiled, then tucked a wayward curl behind my ear.

"Fire away then," he said as he took my hand and rubbed the pad of his thumb over my palm, which immediately soothed my stress.

I took a breath, then exhaled slowly. "I have a hunch there's something we missed when we met Belle. Something huge. Something I should have seen."

"She worked for an alien worshipper society, as you called it, and she knew Jonathan. We should have realized then she wasn't as she seemed. Add in the fact she's related to your mom..."

I laughed quietly. "The fact that Belle is Winston McConnell II's daughter only makes her my mom's fourth cousin or something. Actually, Hope is also related to my mom if she's descended from Daniel, who is Mom's great-great-great-grandfather's brother."

"Anyway, she must have also believed her father when he told Jonathan about the gold, and she's roped Hunter in to believing it too. The map your mom gave to Belle was a fake, but Belle doesn't know that, so I don't know what's going to happen now. I assume she'll come to Luckland to look for the gold."

"Isn't that dicey? The moment she steps foot in Luckland, she risks someone recognizing her. Hunter can't come back either."

Devon nodded. "True, but from what she said when she had Simon and me tied up, she's determined to find that gold. She said it's her birthright."

"The posse's birthright too, though we don't see them searching for gold."

"Unless they already know where it is."

That hypothesis was something Devon and I had discussed some time ago when the ladies seemed determined to dig up the yard at the Manor, but whenever Devon and I had tried to broach the subject with the posse, we were met with tight-lipped glares.

Devon nodded toward the women all hunched together and whispering in the center of the plane. "You know what, Pip? I think we need to really push them to tell us what they know about the gold, and this time, we won't take no for an answer."

CHAPTER EIGHTEEN

The whole town turned out the day my dad and Trey returned with the Alfettas. I'd have thought a circus was coming to town the way everyone lined up and down the sidewalks of Main Street.

Babs stood with Tom in front of the storefront of the building that housed his office, Leah on his shoulders, waving a checkered flag. Hilda and Finn had set up a refreshment stand in front of the Inn and café, while Dani and I plopped into some folding chairs in front of the antique shop. My mom, Matilda, and the rest of the ladies had all gathered at a makeshift seating area in front of the bookstore.

My mother and Matilda had jumped into action when my dad called, saying they were only hours away, and apart from Devon and Simon, who had taken off a little earlier with an errand to run, the entire town had assembled just in time for Dad and Trey's arrival. Louise was also there, but she stood behind the window of Dory's Designs, which was right next door to Tom's office. She kept pulling the curtain aside and peeking out. Perhaps she was miffed that the town seemed to be in a celebratory mood while she'd just lost a sister.

Trey leaned out the passenger window of the truck's cab and waved a checkered flag, just like Leah's. My dad drove, and when he got right in the center of town, he stopped. Didn't even pull over, just stopped. Everyone rushed over, waiting for him to get out and open the trailer.

My mom circled around the front of the truck to the driver's door and waited until my dad got out. He threw his arms around her and kissed her as if he were a sailor returning from duty. I stared at their obvious affection, and it called me to question why they lived apart. Once this parade was over, I was going to have a little tête-à-tête with the parental units.

"Now then, I'm sure you're wondering why I asked you to come here." My mother stood on her back patio in front of Dani, Devon, Babs, and me, hands behind her back.

She was right about me wondering why she'd summoned us. When I received her text, I'd thought she might want me to explain the "news" Devon and I had dangled in front of her and Matilda to get them to return to Luckland. Instead, when I'd arrived at her house, I'd found Devon, Dani, and Babs, who must have received the same text I had. The posse were nowhere in sight. Relief had flooded me, but now, as I stared at my mom, confusion took its place.

"Well, I certainly am," I said. "What's going on?"

"I need you all to follow me. No questions," she said. "Just follow."

I glanced at the others, then shrugged and followed her from the patio and through the house until we reached the downstairs hall closet. Babs kept darting looks at me as if I knew something she didn't. I hadn't got a clue.

My mom opened the door to the closet, then moved all the

coats aside and removed a tall pictureless frame that had leaned against the back closet wall for as long as I could remember. Behind the frame was a full-size door. A secret door. Before I had a chance to ask her where the door led, she knocked on it. It opened.

I blinked when my dad grinned from the other side. "Dad? What's going on?"

My mom smiled. "Just follow. No questions, remember. We'll tell you everything in a minute."

My dad stood back to allow us into a tiny room that barely held all of us, and in the center of the room was a trapdoor— identical to the one Devon had found in our house. Our trapdoor led to nothing more than an old-fashioned cold storage box, but I had a suspicion my dad's led somewhere else. From the way Devon squeezed my fingers, he had the same idea.

Dad strode over to the trap door, then pulled on the large brass handle to lift the heavy piece of flooring to expose a fully lit stairwell. We followed him down the stairwell, which wasn't damp and musty but dry and inviting. At the bottom was a basement without large spiderwebs or scurrying creatures. The walls were bare concrete with nothing but an arched doorway on one wall, leading to who knew where.

"Where does..."

My mom shook her head. "Patience, Pippa."

CHAPTER NINETEEN

My dad's hallway was as familiar to me as Mom's, though I'd never realized we could access his through a secret corridor between the houses.

"Why have you never told us about this underground passage?" I demanded, unable to keep my questions to myself any longer. "Why the secrecy?"

"Precisely my question," Babs said. She stood close to me as if showing solidarity—a rarity from my sister at times.

Dad, ever the peacemaker, held up a hand. "What say we all go out back and have a nice cold brew and discuss all this."

I didn't respond, nor did I wait for anyone else to. I turned on my heel and strode through my dad's house to the patio. When the others had made themselves comfortable and everyone looked calm and rational, I went for the jugular. "The whole separate living quarters thing. It's a sham, isn't it?"

"Not exactly a sham, Pippa, more of a façade," Dad said.

"Why?" Babs was quite shocked. I reached over and grabbed her hand for support.

"Because it was the only way to protect the gold."

Gold? Luckland's legendary gold?

I nearly had a coronary. Babs gasped, and Dani went a little pale.

"You know where it is then?" Devon kept his voice well-modulated, but he had to be shocked even though he and I knew the founders had discovered gold a hundred and seventy years ago.

"Of course we do, and it's long past time you all knew as well. It's a burden to have this knowledge, this responsibility. But we've shielded you as long as we can." My mother turned to my father, her eyes signaling he take over.

My dad reached into his shirt pocket, pulled out a piece of paper, unfolded it, and laid it flat in the center of the table.

We all stared at the map. I'd never seen this one. I'd seen the fake star navigation map they kept in the town hall, but this was different.

"Dev, is this same as the one you took from your mom's house?" I whispered so the others couldn't hear.

"No," he replied just as quietly. "This looks nothing like it."

My mom grinned, obviously overhearing us. "Devon, that map we presumed you took for safekeeping was a fake."

Devon frowned. "Another one?"

"Yes. We have several around town just in case someone like Belle tried to threaten us the way she did. This is a plat map that tells us how the settlers plotted Luckland." She placed a fingertip on what appeared to be the location of the Luckland Inn. "The homes behind the Inn, as you can see, are labeled. Read them."

The print was small but legible. This seemed to be a copy of a copy of a copy. Nothing original about it if she were putting her fingers all over it. I picked up the paper and looked closely. "The first one says L. McDonald." I looked up at my mom, waiting for clarification.

"Go on."

"The next one says S. O'Connor. Then D. Murphy, then S. Murphy. These are the four founders. The fifth house says J. Murphy. That's Dad's house."

"Exactly. Dani, you and your mother are descended from Seamus O'Conner, as is Prudence. Devon, you are descended from Logan McDonald. Pippa and Babs, as you know, are descended from Sean Murphy."

"And Hope is descended from Daniel Murphy. We know, Mother," Babs said. "What has that got to do with the map?"

My mom pursed her lips. "This map is the original town map. Drawn up after everyone had settled in and built their homesteads."

"The founders' houses are all connected. Sean Murphy built a house for his son James. Can you all guess why?" My dad looked at each of us, and I assumed he hoped one of us could guess.

I decided to be the brave one. "Because that house covers the mine entrance." Everyone seemed a bit stunned by my response. "What, are you surprised the mine entrance is here? Or maybe you're just surprised I could figure it out!"

Devon bit back a smile, but there was laughter in his eyes.

"A little of both, actually," Babs said dryly. "So, we're all sitting here on top of a gold mine?"

"That about sums it up," replied my mom.

CHAPTER TWENTY

Devon lay lengthwise on the sofa as I snuggled in next to him, which was probably my most favorite way to snuggle with his arms around me, his palms splayed on my stomach, and him gently tapping his fingers. Simon and Dani had the loveseat but weren't quite so snuggly.

Babs had gone home, but Dani, Devon, and I had gone back to the Manor after my mom and dad's revelation.

"So, let me get this straight," Simon said. "Luckland's legendary gold actually exists, and the mine is beneath the posse's houses, correct?"

I nodded. My parents had explained our ancestors had sealed the mine due to unknown circumstances, but the ladies, who all knew about the mine, didn't want anyone else knowing for several reasons. First and foremost, they didn't want their houses demolished, which would happen if word got out about the gold. Secondly, greed could do terrible things to people. Learning of the mine and how the Murphy clan had to split their time between two houses, however, wasn't what had my mind ticking.

"The map Devon took is a fake, and so is the map my mom

gave to Belle, yet I clearly heard her mention the four winds. What was she raving about?"

Devon sighed. "I have no idea. She'd already started grilling us about entrances and needing four winds, but we couldn't answer her because we didn't know."

"Was she going to shoot you?" I asked, unable to hide the tremor in my voice. Devon tightened his arms around me, then slowly sat up, taking me with him.

"Don't worry about that. The woman is obviously mad."

I'd worry about Devon getting shot for the rest of my life. "Okay, but what's her connection with Lois? The phone threat said if the ladies didn't hand over the map, the cars would end up like Lois. The same voice threatened the ladies last year and said they knew all the ladies' secrets. That has to be Belle because we know she was after the map. So, are we saying she, or Hunter, caused Lois's death?"

"Technically, we don't know if Lois was murdered. Her death was ruled as natural causes," Devon said. "So, unless we find out otherwise, let's table that."

"What I don't understand is how you two got yourselves taken hostage," Dani asked.

Simon grinned. "Rooky error. We walked into the garage because we'd scouted the property and thought nobody was there. Hunter caught us by surprise. The idiot didn't take our phones off us though, which was how we managed to send out our SOS."

"You're lucky Dani could figure out those numbers meant you were in Grand Isle," I said. "The ladies had already discovered where the cars were headed, and their phone call told them to head to Vermont and bring the map, so we put two and two together and realized what had happened. The texts took a little longer to understand, however."

Devon laid his hand on my thigh. "But you did figure it all out, and we're grateful you turned up."

I chuckled. "Dani's SEALs friends helped with their helicopter."

Dani laughed. "They owed me a favor. Don't worry. They'd do the same again if need be."

"Let's hope there isn't another reason for you to call in a favor like that," Simon said, a little bite to his tone.

I hid a smile at his show of jealousy, though Dani seemed oblivious.

I cleared my throat. "So, what's our plan of attack? Belle is still on the loose, and if she wants that gold as much as she seems to, she'll turn up in Luckland."

Devon nodded. "I reckon Hunter will be with her. At first, I thought he was just a hired gun, but after witnessing them in the garage, there's something more going on between them, and I don't just mean she was behind him 'haunting' the Manor. Remember the name of the film company that hired Hunter and Morgan to make that paranormal film BMC? Belle McConnell Chantelle."

Damn. I hadn't figured that out, but it didn't surprise me that she was behind the supposed filming. "We need to find a way to stop her."

"Agreed," Simon said, leaning forward, hands clasped between his knees. "There's only one way to catch a thief."

"Beat them at their own game," Devon said.

"I have it," I murmured. "Founders' Day. They won't be able to resist."

"You mean you think they'll join the annual gold hunt?" Simon nodded. "I can see them trying to blend in with all the other gold hunters. What day is it this year?"

"I don't think the ladies have picked one," Dani said. "But if they find out what we want to do, they'll love it. So, who wants to tell them?"

"Oh, please, allow me." Simon grinned at Dani. "They'll love me all the more for this one."

The ladies did love Simon.

<hr>

Sunday morning at Matilda's was typically a casual brunch. This particular Sunday, the entire posse turned up, along with Babs, Tom, Dani, Simon, and Hilda. Though by this point, Hilda was a de facto member of the Luckland Ladies Society.

We had a bit of a rocky start when Hilda bit into a bagel and popped a crown. On her front tooth. She discreetly held a napkin to her mouth, and when she pulled it away, she grinned. An incredibly awkward few seconds of silence followed, broken only by a snort of laughter from Hilda herself.

"Come on, it's funny. Admit it."

That set Marcy and Hope off into peals of laughter, which set off the rest of us. Once we'd dwindled to a few giggles and dried our tears, we got down to business.

"So, what's this stroke of genius, Simon?" my mom asked, trying to compose herself. "You said it was perfect."

"It is. What do you think of luring a few uninvited gold-digging murderous thieves to your annual Founders' Day cele-bration?" Simon smiled broadly knowing the reaction he'd get. "The celebration will provide Belle and Hunter the opportunity to come into town and hunt for gold, just like everyone else. Except she'll have the fake map that Kate gave her."

"Say no more," Matilda said, holding up her hand. "It's perfect. Simon, you are brilliant."

"Not me." Simon nodded at me. "This was all Pippa's idea."

"Well, then, Pippa, you've outdone yourself." Mom's praise made me smile.

"The question is when?" Prudence asked. "Since we're already planning something for the Fourth of July, I think that should work beautifully."

My mom narrowed her eyes. "But that's only a week away. Not enough time."

"Jasmine called just this morning from the Gazette. The Fourth of July flyer proof is ready, but since we haven't printed them, we'll just slap on a Founders' Day banner and some teaser photos!" Hope turned to me. "Pippa, get out your camera. If we get them to Jasmine by three tomorrow, we'll be fine. We'll need shots of mysterious locations in and around Luckland to mislead the gold diggers."

"You mean tourists, don't you?" I asked, smirking.

"Potayto Potahto," Hope replied with a grin.

Prudence cleared her throat. "I'll organize the tourist maps. Devon, can you devise a plan to capture our miscreants?"

Devon nodded. "Simon and I will sort out something with the sheriff." He glanced at Martin. "I assume you'll want in on the arrest too?"

"That woman threatened the woman I love. I'll not let that go unpunished," Martin said with a smile toward Prudence, who preened.

I stood. "Then, if that's sorted, I'm off. I need to get those photos taken. Anyone care to come along?" I looked pointedly at Devon, hoping he'd take the hint. We still hadn't had any alone time, and I sorely needed some. He looked directly back at me, and a slow smile spread across his face as understanding dawned. His eyes flashed, and I knew his answer before he jumped out of his chair.

"Let's go," he whispered, taking my hand in his as he threw

everyone a wave with the other. "How about we start behind the old mill?"

The old mill was Luckland's version of a Lookout Point— that spot in town every couple knows. It was also a spot the two of us had never been to, with each other, anyway.

"I think that might be the perfect spot to begin," I whispered back.

CHAPTER TWENTY-ONE

The forecast for the Fourth of July was for an unseasonably warm day. Over the last week, we'd distributed flyers all over Luckland and at the nearest tourist stops, and we'd placed ads in the Gazette as well as the Denver area papers.

Every town had its own version of an official tourist area. Ours was an old, covered wagon about a mile out of Luckland, which we'd decorated with an enormous banner featuring a pot of gold. We knew from the buzz on social media we'd be getting hordes of tourists ready to find it. There actually *was* a pot of gold. Each year, the town council bought gold nuggets from a dealer, then placed them in a location indicated on the map. There had to be something for someone to take home. If we attracted enough visitors to Luckland, they'd return next summer. Sure, we were trying to catch a couple of criminals this year, but we still had to maintain our town's objective—to increase tourism, have fun, and commemorate our founders.

Devon and my first stop that morning was Prudence's house. She'd had over a thousand maps printed. Most people would follow the clues we provided and end up on Main Street in front of the newly opened theater. There, new clues would lead them to the park at the end of Main Street, where it would be up to the individual to figure out just where they could find the gold.

I'd expected everyone at Pru's to be on tenterhooks. I did not expect to find the ladies holding flags and drinking mimosas, and the men out back, smoking cigars.

"Why is Hilda dressed like Uncle Sam?"

"It's a great disguise?" Devon tried hard not to laugh. I tried hard not to roll my eyes.

"Don't you think they're celebrating prematurely?" I asked Devon.

"More than likely. I suppose one of us should take things in hand?"

"You suppose correctly, oh wise one. You first."

"Watch this," he said, winking at me as he pulled a plastic whistle out of his pocket and blew in it.

"Oh my god, Devon, is that the whistle you had as a kid? The one you used to blow in my ear?"

He grinned at me.

"Seriously?" I tried to understand how a man could be so hot, so alpha, so smart, and yet regress so easily into a mischievous little boy.

Of course, the whistle worked, and everyone quickly gathered in Prudence's sunken living room.

Devon stood at the fireplace. "If I could have everyone's attention? We've got some decisions to make. Because Belle will try to hide among the tourists, we expect her to follow the clues to the theater first, then sheer off in a different direction. She'll be looking for clues of a different kind. Like people standing guard at a mine entrance. People she'll recognize."

"Who?" I asked.

"Simon and me," Devon said.

I gasped. I did not want Devon in the line of fire again. When I glanced up at him, he smiled softly.

"It's what I do, Pip. It's who I am."

I tried not to show any fear, though my heart raced a mile a minute. "Don't make me save you again," I said in warning, my smile watery.

"You won't need to. We have deputies scattered around town. Once Belle and Hunter are away from the main group of tourists, we'll swoop in and arrest them for theft, kidnapping a police officer and a federal agent and holding them at gunpoint, and any other charges we can level. We've got it covered."

"And what do the rest of us do? While you're playing heroes and villains?" I asked, trying to control my fear with a dose of anger.

"I'm so glad you asked, Pippa." Matilda handed me a sparkly cane and a red, white, and blue glittery top hat. She then handed the same to Dani, Babs, and Morgan—which had me doing a doubletake. *Morgan?*

"Devon," I whispered, waiting for everyone to start chatting so nobody would hear me. "What is Morgan doing here?"

"Morgan suspected Hunter was doing something illegal and handed in some evidence that corroborates Hunter's involvement with the stolen cars."

"What if it's all a ruse, and she's trying to scam us?" I gnawed my lip nervously.

Devon smiled at me. "Morgan didn't know for certain if the evidence would be helpful, but I doubt she would have offered up anything if she were in league with him."

"Does that mean I have to be nice and feel sorry for her?"

He smiled. "Probably."

"If she lays a hand on you, all bets are off, buster." I meant it too.

When Matilda came back my way, she was grinning. It didn't bode well.

"Tillie, what are you up to?"

Matilda passed me a shopping bag, and I shook my head. I knew what I'd find. It was probably a leftover outfit from the old marching band days. Or worse yet, some sort of sequined leotard in royal blue with fishnet stockings from Hilda's *Feingold's Follies Fourth of July Spectacular*. I peeked in the bag to confirm my worst nightmare, then watched as Matilda gave Babs, Dani, and Morgan similar bags.

I shook my head. "No. Just no."

"If I wear this, will you all stop treating me like the town harlot?" Morgan asked, her face flushed.

"Morgan, if you put that on, it won't be us you have to worry about," I replied.

"Look, Hunter is a first-rate jackass, and I feel stupid enough. Putting on this costume can't make things any worse. Perhaps it might offer some redemption."

I could understand her wanting to make amends, and if she was willing to go this far... "Okay, I'm in."

Dani grinned. "I'm in."

"Babs?" I looked at my sister and dared her to say no.

CHAPTER TWENTY-TWO

 at the edge of town. Their ritual was supposed to stop the spirits of those buried in and around Luckland from rising and causing mayhem for the residents of the town—which definitely wasn't working if the increased sightings of ghosts in Luckland were anything to go by. Last year, the women had seemed anxious about doing the ritual. This year, they'd practically dragged their feet, muttering about the shoeboxes the Taos police still had in their possession.

A year ago, I hadn't believed in ghosts or the ritual the women did. I had assumed they performed their ceremony because it gave them some kind of status in Luckland—well, more than they already had. After I'd experienced several apparitions, including the Scarlet Lady at the Inn, I'd changed my mind about ghosts, and I was also quickly changing my mind about the ritual. If something in those shoeboxes was supposed to help keep the spirits at bay as the ladies had hinted, then there was a real reason to get them back.

Cozied up in my kitchen, I glanced at Babs, Dani, and Morgan. Even though the four of us initially agreed to don the silly chorus line getups and attract attention in town, we'd ditched the idea and decided to hold a little planning session of our own.

"So, we assume Belle will follow the map my mom gave her, but if Belle decided it was a fake, like the one at town hall, she might just try to find the mine entrance another way. She mentioned the four winds. Anyone heard of it?" I asked.

Morgan nodded. "Hunter mentioned something about it. He said his financial backer had instructions she found among her father's possessions. The instructions had to do with Luckland's gold, but it didn't say where the gold was. Hunter had an idea the mine entrance was near the Manor. That was why he'd tried to frighten everyone away." Her voice softened at that last bit because she'd been complicit in trying to fool everyone that ghosts haunted the Manor. Little did she know. They did.

"So, you think Belle will search around here?" I asked. Morgan didn't know the mine existed, of course. She just knew Hunter and Belle thought it did.

"When Hunter wasn't pretending to be the perfect boyfriend, he used to doodle a lot on my scratch pad I keep for home decorating ideas. It annoyed the hell out of me because he ended up drawing over my diagrams. He treated my ideas as less than, ya know."

"I didn't know you were into interior design, Morgan," Babs said. "We should compare notes sometime."

That brought a smile to Morgan's face. "Anyway, I'm sure his doodles were tunnels of some sort."

"Do you think you could emulate them?" Dani grabbed a notepad and pencil from my new desk. Not actually new, just new to me. One of those fabulous antique pieces I "borrowed" from the shop.

Dani laid the pad and pencil down on the counter in front of

Morgan. She raised her brows. "You do remember I flunked art sophomore year?"

"Oh, please, that's because you drew the model without his clothes." Babs started laughing as she remembered.

"Model? It was Tommy Thistle. Some model. Plus, I gave him way more credit, you know. He wasn't that well-equipped."

"Is anyone?" Dani asked.

I smiled and raised an eyebrow.

We all laughed, and I wondered whether I'd been holding a grudge against Morgan for all the wrong reasons. It only took her a few minutes to sketch and then she leaned back so we could get a look at the grouping of tubular shapes and little squares.

Babs reached out with a finger and pointed at one of the boxes. "We're here. This is the Manor."

I tipped my head, trying to see what she saw. "Damn, you're right. Those other boxes are the posse's houses."

Morgan pointed to a tiny circle close to where the Manor stood. "And that, according to Hunter, is the entrance to the mine."

I frowned. "The goat house?"

The sudden bleating outside startled us all.

"What in god's name was that?" Morgan asked.

"That was Billy."

"Billy?"

"Yes, he's our pygmy goat. We have two. Billy and Skye. Skye's bleats have more of a screech to them. Come on. I'll show you." I headed out the back door. Billy bounced up to greet me, and I petted his little head.

"Pippa? What are you doing here?"

I turned to find Devon right behind me. "What's going on? I thought you were watching out for... Oh, you think she'll come here too."

"You knew she'd come here?" Devon demanded.

"Well, no, not until Morgan said Hunter thought the mine entrance was here."

He drew in a deep breath. "You all need to go back to town. You'll draw attention to us. We've got this covered."

"Why can't we stay? We'll hide in the house. Maybe we can help." I wanted to see Belle get what she deserved. Dani, Babs, and Morgan, who all stood next to me, nodded in agreement.

"No. Head into town. Hang out at the café. This won't take long. I promise."

"You don't know that, Sherlock. You don't even know if she's coming."

"She's already here," Simon said as he approached us.

"Go. Now." Devon and Simon gave us their best *don't you dare argue* looks, then turned to head inside the house.

"Let's go," I said in a normal tone for the benefit of the boys. Then I lowered my voice. "We'll walk up to that crop of trees. We can hide there and watch."

"You don't think those two will be watching us from the window?" Babs asked. It seemed she didn't have much faith in me.

"Probably. We'll pretend we're taking a shortcut back to town."

Babs rolled her eyes but kept her mouth shut. We needed to be stealthy. If Belle, Hunter, and whoever else showed up, they'd have guns and could harm our boys. We couldn't let that happen.

We crossed the street, then turned into a narrow path that cut into the alley behind the café's old building.

Babs fidgeted. "Why do you think Belle is already here?"

"She must have decided to start searching while everyone was busy setting up," I said.

"She's taking a big risk. What if you'd been home?" Dani asked.

I pushed that thought aside because I didn't like the idea of Belle catching Devon unawares as she'd done in Grand Isle. "Morgan, when did you figure out Hunter was up to no good?" I felt bad that Hunter had played her for a fool.

"I suspected when the cars disappeared. Along with Hunter. Then I found a receipt on the floor of my car for a transport company. I gave it to Devon."

"Wait, Devon knew?"

"Yeah, didn't he tell you?"

"No." I had to bite my tongue for fear of going on a tirade and storming home. "So, the conversation I overhead in the kitchen was confirmation of what they already knew. Unless... When did you give that to him?"

"Um, the night before you all took off to Grand Isle. I would have thought Devon would have told you, Pip. I'm sorry. He seems like such a great boyfriend. Honest and all." Morgan seemed wistful.

"He has his flaws, Morgan. Secrets being one of them." I sighed. There would be time for recriminations later because Belle and Hunter had arrived.

CHAPTER TWENTY-THREE

We'd found a perfect stakeout point behind the trees. We could see straight across the street with a perfect view of the side and backyard of the Manor. I didn't know what surprised me more—Belle and Hunter blatantly walking up to the Manor, map in hand as if they were sure they wouldn't get caught, or their disguise.

Belle wore a red, white, and blue jogging suit and a blue sparkle eye mask. Hunter also wore the patriotic jogging suit and eye mask, though he'd covered his hair using a top hat just like Hilda's. I had no idea what made them think those disguises could hide them from Luckland's law enforcement.

"They must think everyone's in town," Dani whispered, trying her best not to snort with laughter.

I had to bite the inside of my cheek before I could talk. "They look ridiculous. How long will the boys wait before nabbing them?"

Morgan's expression was a cross between shock and mortification. I thought she was shocked at such a sight and mortified she'd actually dated him.

"Morgan, we've all been there. No regrets. No looking back. Chalk it up to hormones and move on," I told her.

"Easy for you, Pippa. You got the prize." Morgan sighed and shook her head.

"Look, once this is over, we'll have a girl's night to ease the pain. Right, girls?" I looked at Dani and Babs for confirmation. Both smiled and nodded. "Good, okay, back to business. How long do we give them before we nab them ourselves?"

Dani tapped my shoulder. "Shh. There they go."

Belle and Hunter snuck along the side of the house toward the gate leading to the back pasture where the goat house stood. I watched, transfixed, waiting to see how long it would take for the boys to burst out the back door and yell "freeze." Seconds ticked by excruciatingly slowly. Literally. Babs's new smartwatch with the ticking seconds annoyed the hell out of me.

Hunter opened the gate, and Belle pushed him through before she quickly followed and closed the gate behind her. They reached into their pockets, but I was too far to see what they were doing.

That was when Simon and Devon chose to appear. Each came around from the back of the shed, arms outstretched, gun in their hands. At least, I assumed they were guns. From that distance, I only saw the sun glint off something.

The boys yelled. Probably told Belle and Hunter to freeze— just as Billy and Skye came charging from behind the house. When they got to Belle and Hunter, the little goats reared and kicked the kidnapping thieves, knocking them on their asses. Before they could scramble and get back up, our incredibly adorable pair of pygmies continued to jump up and down as if playing, their hooves just missing Belle and Hunter. Simon and Devon stood motionless. They must have been in awe of the frolicking bovids.

I took off running across the road, and when I reached the gate, I called for Billy and Skye. I knew Devon and Simon couldn't cuff the lawless duo until the goats were out of the way. I was so proud of those two. Not the boys, the goats. I reached into the bucket I kept nearby with their pine branch treats and rewarded them handsomely.

"Good boy, Billy," I whispered as I scratched between his ears. I turned to Skye. "Hello, my darling girl. Aren't you the brave one." I gave her a few scratches too.

I looked over as Devon and Simon pulled Belle and Hunter off the ground. Devon read them their rights as the girls charged across the street, Morgan out front, leading the way. She looked ready to burst.

The moment Hunter saw her, he breathed a sigh of relief. "Morgan, oh thank god. I need you to call my attorney. His number is on my fridge. Key is in my pocket."

Morgan just stood looking at him.

"Babe? Come on, come over here and grab the key."

"Not in a million years, Hunter, and in case you haven't realized… We're over."

"What? What the hell, Morgan?"

"Stop whining, Hunter," Belle demanded. "You realize we're all here. We have the four winds. We just need to call upon them."

Hunter glanced around. "Where?"

Belle looked at us, her mask still covering her eyes. "There are three right there. Pippa, her sister, and her friend. Add me, and you have four. We can open it." She turned back to Devon and Simon. "We have to try, at least. Just let me walk over to it with those three, and we'll see."

"Belle, you do realize there is no mine. No gold. What your father told you was nothing but a legend—"

"No. It's real, I tell you. How can you all just stand there? We can open it."

Devon suddenly looked past my shoulder and took a few steps toward the gate. "Here comes Marty and the ladies."

I turned, and sure enough, the Luckland Ladies marched across my front lawn in perfect time to the band warming up on Main Street.

My mother stopped short as soon as she was close enough to see Belle. The others barreled right into her.

"Why aren't they in the back of a squad car?" my mom asked, eyes blazing.

"We were just about to call in the troops," Simon said, holding up his phone.

"Looks like they're already here," I murmured, which earned an elbow in my ribs from Dani.

"Humph." Matilda shoved her way to the front of the group. "Well, what are you waiting for?"

"She wants to try to open the entry door to the mine," Babs said, her tone snarky.

"She wants us to all stand here and break wind," I said, barely concealing my laughter.

"Here?" Hope asked, looking around the empty pasture.

Belle's face turned red. "The mine is here. I know it is. You bitches can't fool me."

The ladies all glanced at one another and seemed to have a silent conversation. My mother nodded, then turned to Belle. "Okay. Have at it."

"We need to head to the goat house," Belle said.

Devon escorted Belle over. I pulled Dani by one arm and Babs by the other.

"Could someone take off this mask? I'm going to have raccoon eyes soon." She was awfully demanding for a criminal about to be hauled off to jail, but Devon agreeably removed her mask.

"Oooh, you were right. That blue glitter does make you look a bit raccoonish," I said, which earned a beady scowl from Belle.

"Well, we're all here, Belle. Now what?" Matilda crossed her arms over her chest and glared.

"Watch." Belle lifted her head toward the sky and began chanting. "Oh, winds of the East, West, North, and South bring us your strength. Open the gates for the golden ones." Her voice was singsongy and incredibly off-key.

She kept her face tilted toward the sun, around her eyes sparkling with glitter. A minute or two went by.

"Looks like that only works in Oz, Belle." My mother was in quite the sarcastic mood, but I didn't really blame her.

"Stuff it, Kate," Belle replied before she looked up again. "Oh, spirit of the winds that guard the blessed treasure within the earth. Open your gates and lead us inward."

Another minute passed. Still nothing.

"I was so sure," Belle muttered.

"Well, as fun as that was, I'm afraid we're going to have to head down to the station," Simon said before he and Martin led the two criminals out of the yard.

"I'll follow them over to the station and wrap things up. Then we can all enjoy the celebration." Devon smiled at everyone, then gestured with his hands to usher us away.

"Devon, I don't have to leave. It's my house," I reminded him.

"Ours, Ms. forget-me-not. *Our* house. And you do. This is a crime scene."

CHAPTER TWENTY-FOUR

"I don't feel this is over. Belle knew far too much about all of us and this town. Things she couldn't know."

The posse, along with Dad, Babs, and Dani, sat on my dad's back patio. Devon and Simon had once again disappeared to parts unknown. Devon had the nerve to tell me they were going fishing. On a Monday. Plus, he said it with a smirk. He was up to something, the sneaky devil.

My mother frowned. "Such as?"

"Such as when I spoke to her about that little silver box I found in the shop. She said it would suit the antique shop. How did she know I worked at an antique shop? I hadn't told her. She also knew about the cars. That's not public knowledge. Also, we know Belle was behind both phone threats, so I think we've been looking at this all wrong. We've believed whoever knew your secrets had gotten them from one of the missing shoeboxes, but as Belle made those threats, she already knew your secrets."

From the glances the ladies gave one another, I'd hit the nail on the head.

"Devon said she won't talk," Matilda said. "She only

admitted to demanding the map. She blamed Hunter for stealing the cars."

"I have an idea," I said. "I'm going to do a little sleuthing. Babs, Dani, I'll need your help." I turned to my sister and my friend and waited for their agreement.

Dani smiled. "I'm in."

Babs nodded. "What do you need?"

Getting Hope and Marcy to share their files at the Luckland Inn didn't take much convincing. By Friday, we had hunkered down in the back office of the Inn. The five of us divided up the files. Babs, Dani, and I took half. Marcy and Hope, the other half.

"What exactly are we looking for?" Marcy asked.

"I'm positive Belle's been to Luckland. I just don't know when. This is the only place in town for visitors to stay. My guess is she had to have been here a long time ago. Whether she used her real name or not, I don't know."

"Wait. This is silly," Hope said suddenly. "Let me scan the ledgers into the computer. Then we just hit search and let the computer do the work. It takes a while, but no longer than us manually going through them. Leave the books there, and I'll call you when I'm done."

"I should have thought of that, Hope. Sorry." Though now, Dani, Babs, and I could begin the other side of our investigation. Hunter.

We headed through the partition doors in the lobby of the Inn to the café and grabbed a table in the back. It was early enough that coffee and a croissant sounded pretty good—along with a chat with Morgan.

The café was fairly empty as the breakfast crowd had cleared out, and virtually all the Founders' Day visitors had finally departed. No sense hanging around after someone had found the pot of gold.

We asked Morgan to join us for a moment and pulled up a fourth chair. Surprisingly, Babs began the inquisition.

"Morgan, did Hunter ever mention where he grew up?"

Morgan thought for a moment, then pursed her lips. "Actually, on our first date he told me he grew up in Boulder. But then in another conversation, I mentioned the hot air balloon festival in New Mexico, the one your grandparents died at. He said he watched it every year as a kid. Said it was only a few hours from his house. That didn't strike me as odd until later, when I realized he was a scurvy-faced lying scumbag."

"We know Belle grew up in New Mexico, but I don't see how that's a solid connection to Hunter. We still need to figure out how they met each other," Dani said.

I nodded. Devon had said he didn't think Hunter was simply a hired gun, that there was something more between Hunter and Belle. After witnessing them together, so did I. "Did Hunter ever mention Belle?" I asked Morgan.

She shook her head. "No. I had no idea who she was until Devon told me she and Hunter had held Devon and Simon at gunpoint. Devon questioned me about Hunter's involvement with her, but the best I could do was explain that Hunter had a financial backer who asked him to find the gold mine—which we now know was Belle."

The door to the kitchen in the back suddenly swung open, and Hope marched in, excitement all over her face as she slapped several pieces of paper down on our table and spread them out.

"Bingo. B. I. N. G. O."

We all peered at the printouts.

I frowned. "I don't see Belle's name anywhere, Hope."

Hope pointed to one printout. "Line thirteen." Pointing to

the next, she said, "Line eight." Then she pointed to the last two pages. "Line two and nine."

"That says Mattie McConnell," Dani said.

"Holy Macaroons! McConnell. She used her real name!" Looking around the café, I realized we'd drawn a few gazes. I grinned. "What are the dates?"

Hope pulled up a chair and sat down. "It appears she stayed at the Inn in eighty-nine, ninety-one, then again in ninety-four. And...look at this." She pointed to the last printout. "Remember the furry convention at Thanksgiving last year?"

"Like anyone could forget," Babs murmured.

I tried not to laugh because that was when a furry had accidentally knocked a green gelatinous salad over her head, ruining her white jumpsuit.

"Well, she was there then too. In costume," Hope said.

"I bet she was the moose," Dani declared.

Babs grinned. "More likely the ass."

I shook my head. "Regardless of what costume she wore, she's been to Luckland several times. So, now we have to figure out what she was up to."

"Not without me, you don't." Devon's deep and sexy voice came from the doorway. I looked up at him and smiled.

"While you all were busy snooping around, Simon and I were as well. Feel like a road trip?" he asked as he raised a brow.

"With you? Always."

CHAPTER TWENTY-FIVE

The blaring of the RV's foghorn made Devon and me jump. We were just locking up the front door, getting ready to depart, when the infamous Luxmobile, as I fondly called it, pulled up in our drive.

Matilda popped her head out the side window as the door opened. "Come on, the clock's ticking. Let's hit the road."

Devon and I shared a horrified look. We were really looking forward to a little couple's time away from the loony bin. Devon's birthday was just days away, and I thought maybe we could have a private celebration. When Matilda disappeared from the window and Hilda took her place, I knew we were in trouble.

"Come on, Pip. I saved you a seat." *Oh no. No, no, no.*

Prudence sat in the driver's seat, impatiently tapping on the wheel.

"Let's go, Devon. You are *not* making me do this alone!" Simon's voice bellowed out from a rear window. How they got him on board, I hadn't a clue.

Devon and I grudgingly boarded the luxury liner, and as Devon stored our overnight bags in the luggage compartment, I surveyed the scene. "I see Babs must have taken a hard pass," I muttered, noticing her absence, though Dani and her mom were present.

"She and Tom are going to keep a lookout here, along with the menfolk. Someone must," Hilda said a bit too gleefully.

"Aren't Devon and Simon menfolk?" I asked, biting back a smirk.

"Oooh, yes, they are." Hilda popped a brow and winked. "We need a little eye candy on board, don't you think?"

"That's my son you're cackling about," Matilda remarked, scowling.

"Though she does have a point, Tillie," I said, grinning at Hilda.

"We're not here as eye candy," Simon said as he headed toward the passenger seat up front—the one usually reserved for my mother. When he'd gotten comfortable, he turned and gave the women a once-over. "We're here to ensure you don't all land up in the pokey."

After a heartbeat or two of silence, they all burst into laughter. Ice broken, Prudence gunned the engine and took off with a lurch. It was going to be a long trip, so I headed toward my usual seat in the lounge section.

The well-equipped RV could have belonged to a traveling rock star. Seriously impressive with a full kitchen, a full-size restroom dubbed the Lovely Lavatory, a fireplace, internet, and satellite TV. They'd missed nothing on this land boat. Sleeping quarters were available for ten if needed, but they always preferred hotels and RV parks with cabins.

Simon cleared his throat to get attention. "Just to be clear, you ladies cannot go off like rockets around town investigating. You have to follow our lead. You all understand that, right?"

"Oh, absolutely, Simon." My mother oozed sweetness and obedience. "We wouldn't think of operating outside the box."

"I'm not worried about the box, Kate. I'm worried about the town of Roswell surviving your invasion." Simon shook his head, and it was easy to see he hadn't wanted to go on this trip.

I looked at Dani and nodded in his direction. Perhaps if she had a little chat with him, he'd settle down. She took the little pop-up seat behind his and leaned in to whisper something. He turned his head slightly and smiled. I would have loved to be a fly on the windshield just about then. Those two were like twigs of kindling, waiting for a flame to ignite them.

Settling in for the ride, I leaned into the crook of Devon's arm and breathed deeply. Devon always smelled good. Not a particular cologne or aftershave. Just Devon. His heart steadily thumped beneath my ear, lulling me into a light sleep.

"Shake, shake, shake!"

I awoke with a start. "What the hell was that?"

Devon shook with laughter. He cupped my chin and tilted my head toward the front of the RV. I should have known. Matilda and Rosa were singing a disco number on the karaoke machine and shaking their hips.

I laid my head back down on Devon's chest. He ran his fingers through my hair and gently kissed me on the head. "Can't take them anywhere," he said.

I chuckled. "Is it margarita time yet?"

"I'm sure we can scare one up for you. Marcy? Anything left in that pitcher?"

"Coming up."

I eased off Devon and sat upright, stretching my arms. Matilda and Rosa handed off their microphones to my mom and Hope, who were not known for their singing ability. Their voices weren't terrible; they just had an issue with singing in key. Nothing like Abba sung with virtually no harmony.

About an hour later, Prudence switched lanes and took an exit. I craned my neck to see where we were. Las Vegas, New Mexico. Devon and I were quite familiar with the town, and I was more than ready to stop for a bite to eat. I knew just the place.

"Devon, we have to," I said, confident he'd know what I meant.

He grinned. "Say, Prudence, take a left up ahead. There's a fabulous café we can lunch at."

"Lunch at?" I chuckled. He had a way with words, that boy.

During our last visit to Roswell, we'd encountered a situation when we stopped for lunch. The owners of the café, Christopher and his wife Gina, were in labor and needed a hand clearing out the lunch crowd so they could go have a baby. Devon and I were happy to help. On the way home, we stopped off again, and I did a photo session so they could have some memories. I still stayed in touch with them.

They were thrilled to see us but a little surprised we'd brought half of Luckland with us. They quickly assembled a large table and, without bothering with menus, served us huge bowls of pasta and salad, family style. Then they brought their adorable little girl out to meet us. A year old, Francesca was already walking. Cutest little thing. For just a moment, a very, very short moment, I wondered what having a little girl of my own would be like.

Once we'd all piled back in the RV and were on our way to Roswell, I decided to open Pandora's box and question the ladies with something that had bugged me for quite some time.

"I have a question for each of you," I announced as I tapped my fingers nervously on Devon's leg. "What did Lois do to you?"

"We told you, dear," my mom answered quite blithely. "She was very destructive."

I shook my head. "Uh-uh, not this time. I want the skinny. Deets. Now."

My mother sighed and set her mouth in a determined line. "All right then. Prudence? You first." She nodded at Pru, who looked into the rearview mirror and caught my eye.

She focused back on the road. "Simple. Freshman year of high school. First day. Lois sat with the popular girls. I found out later they let her sit there in exchange for gossip. She told them she *heard* I'd lost *it* to some guy I met over the summer. Because of that, I was branded a supreme slut for the rest of my days in high school."

"Wow. So yeah, okay, that was bad. Matilda?"

"She saw me buy my pregnancy test and told every damn customer at the Mercantile who would stop to listen."

"Before you even took the test? Oh, that's wicked. Hope?"

"While in second grade, she told everyone I was adopted. I went home in tears, only to learn it was true."

I could feel her pain through her words.

"Rosa?"

"When we first moved to Luckland, she told everyone I was there illegally. I won't tell you the names people called me."

"Oh, now that's fucked up," Simon said, and he immediately went to give Rosa a hug.

I braced myself. "Mom?"

"My first starring role in a play was the old summer theater at the park. Lois tried out but didn't get the part. Instead, she reviewed it for the local paper. Called me a simpering robot. Said I was miscast as a femme fatale and should have been given the role of wallpaper."

I couldn't grasp how anyone could have been so vicious, but

the ladies' stories finally helped me understand their animosity toward Lois.

As we approached Roswell, Devon stood and headed to the front. He pointed out the window for Prudence. "See that big box hardware store up ahead? Drop Simon and me off there. We're going to rent a truck to buzz around town."

Prudence nodded and pulled into the lot. She came to a stop, then opened the door. Simon headed out, but Devon stopped on the step.

"Now, about a mile back, I saw a sign for an RV park. Copper Penny. Or maybe it was the Wooden Nickel. Whichever, we'll meet you all there."

We made the turn toward the RV park, which was neither the Copper Penny nor the Wooden Nickel. It was called the Brass Tack. The turn also put us on the same route Devon and I had taken to Belle Chantelle's ranch, which I couldn't help but comment on.

"What did you say?" Prudence began to slow the vehicle as we approached the RV park entrance.

"I believe she said *this is the way to Belle's*," Matilda said.

My mom looked at me eagerly. "Do you remember the way?"

"No, no, no. We are not going to Belle's. They've probably got cops crawling all over the place and would be highly suspicious of us."

"Like they've never seen lost tourists before. Puhlease," Hilda said. "Prudence, keep driving. Pippa? How far?"

I chewed my lower lip nervously. This was a terrible idea.

"About a mile." The words just spewed out of my mouth involuntarily—which was how we found ourselves driving through the familiar gates of the Belle Starr Ranch.

CHAPTER TWENTY-SIX

"It's remarkable," Marcy stated once Prudence stopped the RV and cut the engine.

"I'm going with peculiar," Hope said, tilting her head to get a better look.

"Prudence, what say you?" Matilda asked our resident expert on aliens.

"Batshit crazy," Prudence muttered and shook her head. This was from a woman whose roof had not a single flat surface.

"Got that right," Hilda said.

"*Dios Mio*," Rosa whispered before she made the sign of the cross. Rosa hadn't been to church in years.

The first time I'd seen Belle's house, I'd been as stunned as they were now. In fact, I still couldn't understand the architecture, which made the house look like a flying saucer.

"Shh!" Dani hissed. "I just saw someone. Coming around from the back... Look."

In perfect sync, we all moved from the right side of the RV to the left and plastered our faces against the windows.

A big stocky guy in a muscle shirt and high-waisted jeans

headed toward us. The ladies spun into action so fast, I barely caught on to what they were doing.

Prudence turned to Rosa. "Rosa, you take the driver's seat, and when he gets to the RV, open the door and put on a show. Don't let him on though. Just lead him on." Then Prudence took Dani and me by the arms and gave us a nudge. "Go, hide in the back."

Dani made a face at the idea of Rosa leading anyone on other than Dani's dad, but we obediently did as asked. We all squeezed into the back cabin, but we left the door ajar so we could hear.

"*Oh, estoy perdido.*" Rosa's voice was breathy and sexy. "*Estoy buscando el pozo de fuego. No, eso no está bien. ¿Parque de casas móviles de sillas de montar en llamas? ¿Creo? Dios mío, se supone que debo conocer a mi hermana, Angélica, que me va a asesinar. ¿Cómo llego allí?*"

There was no response.

"What'd she say?" I asked Dani.

Dani grinned. "She's looking for the Blazing Saddles RV park, and her sister Angelica is going to kill her. She asked how to get there."

"*Dónde está* RV park? Back that way? *Gracias.*"

I highly suspected the man had no idea what Rosa said, but as she closed the door, Prudence raced up to the front. The man must have turned his back because Rosa and Prudence switched places, and within seconds, Prudence had peeled out of there.

We headed back to the Brass Tack RV park and secured our lodging for the night. Not exactly the luxury RV resort we were hoping for. Nor was it even alien-themed. I would have thought every tourist trap would be alien-themed in Roswell.

"Who do you think that guy was?" I asked as we settled down to wait for Devon and Simon to return. "No idea, but he didn't seem too concerned about us. Maybe he's security?" Dani chuckled because the guy definitely didn't have the security guard vibe.

He obviously worked for Belle, and I wondered if he had anything to do with stealing the cars. It would be interesting to find out. "Maybe. I'd like to know what Devon and Simon are up to. Devon said they'd been snooping, but he didn't tell me what they'd unearthed. I assume it has something to do with the International UFO Artifact Society Belle worked for, the one Winston McConnell II founded."

"What would the alien society have to do with how Belle knew the ladies' secrets?" Dani asked.

I grinned. "She probably got little green men to spy on the posse."

"Don't joke about aliens, Pippa," Prudence said, her tone tight.

I turned to face the woman who had once believed aliens had landed on Earth. "Sorry, Prudence."

She nodded at my apology, and I decided to quickly change the subject. "As you all know, Devon's birthday is in a few days, and I thought I could plan a surprise for him this year."

"Oh dear, you know he's not much for celebrating his birthday," Matilda said.

"I know, but maybe this year is different. Trey is in his life now. Maybe this is the perfect year to celebrate." I really wanted to do something for Devon. "Maybe just a little party at the Inn. How about that?"

"We'll talk about it later," my mother announced, pointing outside. "The man of the hour is arriving."

Just my luck. However, I was indeed excited to see what they'd found.

"What the hell were you all doing at Belle's?" Devon practically bellowed.

"That's not important. What's important, Inspector Oblivious, is that a man who doesn't look like a security guard is wandering around her property. He could have had something to do with stealing the cars. He might give us the dirt on Belle and Hunter, so we can lock them away for longer." I thought he and Simon would be excited at our news. They weren't.

"We told you to come straight here. Do not stop. Do not pass go. Do not go anywhere near Belle Chantelle's ranch."

"You never said any such thing," I replied.

"She's right, son, you didn't." Matilda put a hand on my shoulder in solidarity.

"Shouldn't need to, Red. It's common sense. You could have compromised an ongoing criminal investigation."

"We only drove through the gates, turned around, and came back out. Rosa told the guy she'd gotten lost."

Devon sighed. "We know. We saw you."

I frowned. "You did?"

Simon grinned and dropped quite a large box on the banquette table. "Yes, and thanks for the distraction."

"What's in there?" Matilda asked as all the ladies stood to take a look.

Devon shook his head. "We're not going to open anything till we're well on our way out of here. Prudence, get this thing in gear."

"So, it was all right for you to compromise a criminal investigation but not us?" As soon as I asked the question, I knew the answer. Though they were lawmen, Devon and Simon seemed to skirt the law when it came to helping the ladies.

"Don't mind Pippa," my mom said. "I'm sure you had your reasons."

I shook my head. "Seriously, Mom? You're taking his side?"

She shrugged, then sat when Prudence got the RV underway. I turned back to face Devon. "What about the goon at Belle's?"

"Already on it, Pip. You should have had more faith in me."

I would have had a clever retort, but the box held my attention. "We really have to wait?"

"Trust me," Devon said.

CHAPTER TWENTY-SEVEN

"Who are they from?" I asked as the ladies began digging out old letters from the box Devon and Simon had filched from Belle's house. When Devon had said we had to wait, I didn't think he'd make us wait until we'd gotten home. He'd even made us wait until Babs and Tom had arrived with my dad and Trey. Now, we were just waiting on Martin.

"You won't believe it," Hope said, holding up a letter.

"Try us," Marcy remarked from behind her, unable to grab any for herself.

"Saint Josephine on a cracker," Hilda whispered, grasping one in her hand.

"If she weren't dead already, I'd kill her myself," Prudence announced.

"And I'd be right there with you," said my mom.

"We all would." Matilda looked around my kitchen, then smacked her palm on the table.

I looked at Devon, bewildered. "Lois?" I asked quietly, though clearly the letters must have been from her. "To Belle?" My stomach churned just thinking about what might be in them.

"It appears Lois told Belle every damn thing that went on in this town. For years." My mother was angrier than I'd ever seen her. Angrier, even, than when Babs had accidentally sold off the six shoeboxes over a year ago.

Prudence nodded. "Everything and more. But we don't know the full story, and we won't until we find the letters Belle wrote to Lois."

"Then I guess we better start reading," Martin announced as he strode in carrying several boxes. "Found these at Lois's, along with some other very interesting items. Before we go further... Devon, Simon, can I see you for a moment?"

Martin placed the boxes on the kitchen bench and headed out the back door, Devon and Simon right behind him. The overhead outside light illuminated our shaky little deck, enabling me to read Devon's body language, which changed from relaxed to tense and back to relaxed again.

"Something's up," I murmured.

Babs shook her head. "Clearly. I bet they found something incriminating. Maybe they know who killed Lois."

"Who's Lois, Mommy?"

I'd forgotten Leah had been quietly sitting on the floor, humming and playing with a doll. Oops. "Never mind who Lois is, sweetie. Why don't you and Jasmine go watch your elephant show? I'll turn it on for you."

"Jasmine is afraid of elephants." Leah started pouting, convinced her doll was afraid of everything.

"Actually, Jasmine told me earlier she wouldn't be afraid of them if she knew more about them. So maybe watching the show will help."

Once I had her settled in front of the little TV in the corner of the room, I went back to pondering what the boys were discussing.

Matilda shoved a bunch of letters in my hands. "They'll tell us when they're ready. In the meantime, let's get to these letters. Divvy 'em up. Let's go."

I didn't want to question whether we had any right to read the letters. It seemed more important to find out what they held. A few minutes later, Devon, Martin, and Simon came back in and seemed just as eager to go through the stacks of letters along with the rest of us.

"You know, wouldn't this make more sense if we matched up Lois's letters with Belle's?" Hope asked. "Then we can see how Belle reacted to Lois's gossip?"

"Good idea, Hope. Do we know the earliest correspondence?" Prudence asked. She was a researcher, after all.

"1990 as best I can tell," she replied. "Let's start there. Anyone with ninety, drop your letters here." She pointed to a spot on the left side of the room. "We'll put each consecutive year in order. First Belle's letters, then let's do the same with Lois's in a row beneath." Hope was always very, very meticulous.

We all grabbed our stacks and quickly realized they were already bundled by year. That made it easy. Once we'd placed all Belle's letters in order, which created almost thirty piles, we opened Lois's boxes again. They weren't so neatly bundled, so it took a little longer to sort those out.

"Who's got ninety?" my mother asked because she'd decided to play letter moderator.

"I do," Hilda said.

"Okay, you start. What do we know? Devon, dear, take notes."

Devon looked up in surprise and scowled. Devon didn't like being told what to do. I gently squeezed his leg. He looked at me and sighed in resignation. Holding out his hand, he waited for someone to hand him a scratch pad and pen.

"Mattie McConnell, aka Belle Chantelle, first wrote to Lois

after they met in Luckland in eighty-nine, it seems. Listen to this." Then Hilda began to read.

April 18, 1990

My dearest friend Lois,

I can't thank you enough for your kindness and hospitality during my brief visit to your wonderful town. I'm sorry it took so long to write. Turns out, it wasn't the flu after all. Enclosed, please find a snapshot of my wonderful new surprise. I must ask you not to tell a soul, however. It shall always remain my deepest secret, one I need to share with someone, and I choose you.

"There's no photo or anything in the envelope. Anyone care to guess?" Hilda looked around as if she knew the answer.

"Okay, moving on then."

August 5, 1990

My dearest friend Lois,

It was so good to hear from you. I'm glad Founders' Day was a big success this year, and I am sorry to have missed it. But that is my life nowadays. Can't just pick up and go. Perhaps in a year or two, I shall return.

"And here's the kicker. The reply from Lois." Hilda was smirking.

My dear friend Mattie,

I completely understand your inability to travel for our festival this year, though I did miss you. And trust me, our town is no stranger to your predicament. In fact, one of our very own is in a similar situation. And one of our founding families, no less.

Hilda looked at Matilda, then Devon. "Sorry, I have to keep reading."

Not only that, but I heard it was a lounge lizard in Vegas. Through the grapevine, of course.

"I think you all get the picture," Hilda said.

Devon looked around curiously. "Belle was pregnant when she came to Luckland. And had a baby. Single mom, just like mine. Hiding it, just like mine. Anyone else thinking what I'm thinking?"

A resounding chorus went up. "Hunter."

"Has to be," Simon said. "I'll run the DNA."

"Let's move on," my mom said. "Hope?"

Hope cleared her throat, then began to read.

October 31, 1992

My dearest friend Lois,

Steppenhoffer, that's the professor's name, came back. I had to tell him. He was quite angry, but then he realized what a treasure we had. Winston refuses to acknowledge him.

"Wait… What does she mean, him? Steppenhoffer? Or the baby?"

"Doesn't say," Hope replied. "There's more."

November 11, 1992

My dear friend Mattie,

That is quite odd, I must say. Your professor Steppenhoffer? Little Miss never-a-prude Prudence got married not about eight years ago, her second, by the way, to a professor Steppenhoffer. Can you imagine? What are the odds?

Devon held up his hand. The women were all becoming quite distraught. Prudence looked about ready to blow a gasket. Who could blame them? Lois Thorpe had been spilling secrets to Belle Chantelle who clearly was so entangled in their lives and business that it was horrifying.

"I think we've heard enough to know Belle Chantelle and Lois had quite the friendship, and Belle had more secrets than we imagined," Devon said. "This will take some time to sort through, and I'm afraid I have to take these letters in for evidence. Sorry, but I need you all to let us take them for a thorough analysis."

The room went eerily quiet.

"Wait, Devon," Matilda said suddenly, clasping a letter in her hand tightly.

He nodded for her to continue.

She opened the letter and took a breath.

July 19, 2005

My dearest friend Lois,

You cannot believe how well and how deeply I understand your feelings about Luckland. About being an outsider. I have such news to tell you, and perhaps you can understand it better than anyone. Winston McConnell II has passed away. To my horror, he left me only what we had here in Roswell. Everything else went to Nadia, but I am determined to get it all back. Can you imagine my shame when the will referred to Nadia as his daughter and me as his employee?

"Devon is right. We've heard enough," my mother stated emphatically.

CHAPTER TWENTY-EIGHT

"Happy birthday, Devon!"

The chorus of voices nearly deafened me as the posse marched from the kitchen into the dining room, where I'd set up an elaborate buffet of Devon's favorite foods.

I held my breath and waited for his reaction because he didn't always react predictably.

He looked down at me, his mother, and back at me. Then he grinned. Oh, thank the lord. I didn't want grumpy Devon on his birthday. I wanted happy Devon.

I quickly grabbed a slice of the salami he'd been eyeing and reached up to feed it to him. I didn't know what made the Toscano so special, but Devon certainly did if the bliss on his face as he savored it was any indication.

"That good, eh?" I asked with a smile.

He grabbed a slice and winked. "Open up. You have to try this."

I played the obedient girlfriend and took a bite. He was right. It was delicious. The women all took this as their cue to get the party started. It was suddenly chaos as Babs and her brood traipsed in, followed by Martin, Simon, and Trey, all bearing gifts. I squeezed Devon's hand to keep him grounded. He wasn't accustomed to this kind of focus. In fact, not since he'd first returned to Luckland and became a local hero had he this much attention showered on him. I took the opportunity to slink off and grab my camera to take a few candid shots. Someday, the photos would make a great scrapbook to show our... Well, just to show.

After a few minutes, while I busily took photos, everyone shuffled into the living room and circled something in the middle.

As I spied the object, my face fell. "Please tell me that is not what I think it is."

"That depends, dear. What do you think it is?" My father bellowed with laughter.

Babs grinned. "Looks like a stripper cake, Dad. You know, the ones they have at bachelor parties?" She did her best not to laugh.

I did my best not to scream. My, how the tables had turned.

Devon circled the cake and eyed it curiously with a distinct smirk. Maybe I needed to develop thicker skin, but I hated surprises, and whatever popped out of that cake was going to piss me off—until I noticed who was missing, and I grinned.

"You look way too happy, Pip. What do you know? What's in there?" Devon asked, dropping his smirk.

"Sorry, Detective, no can do. This surprise is all yours." I patted his chest, leaned up, and kissed him. "Happy Birthday," I whispered, still smiling.

I backed away a few steps and held up my camera just as the top of the cake popped off, and the cake girl burst out. Cackling, she stepped down and literally threw herself at Devon. I laughed so hard I could hardly catch my breath.

Devon disentangled himself from the cake girl and backed away, eyes wide, shaking his head.

"Are you all right," I asked.

"A ninety-year-old woman in a sparkly leotard just mauled me. What do you think?"

Babs chuckled. "Look on the bright side. At least she wasn't wearing peekaboo pasties over her... You know?"

Devon turned an odd shade of yellow.

"Okay, no more teasing," I said to him. "Unless we're alone. Let's see what else they've got planned."

"I'm afraid to."

Simon threw his arm about Devon's shoulders and grinned. "I hear strip poker might be in the cards." With that, he slapped Devon on the back and laughed before strolling over to where Dani and Rosa chatted.

"Come on, let's go sit out back." I grabbed Devon's hand and pulled him onto what someday would be an amazing deck, but right now consisted of some shaky boards. "A few minutes away from the crazy would do us some good."

"How long till they all leave?" he asked.

"Not soon enough, so let's make the most of the next two minutes until they hunt you down."

I pointed up. "Oh, look, Dev, a shooting star! Quick, make a wish."

He closed his eyes and smiled. When he opened them, there was a glint to them.

"What did you wish for?"

"Can't tell you, or it won't come true."

"Not even if I pout?"

"Not even then."

"Not even if I kiss you? Here?" I leaned up and kissed the tiny freckle on the side of his neck that always made him shiver.

"Nope."

"Or here?" I kissed the other side of his neck.

"Nope. But fair warning, guests or not, you keep that up, and you'll be fulfilling a whole lot of wishes later." He raised a brow and grinned.

CHAPTER TWENTY-NINE

The moment I entered the living room, I stopped short. Devon gave Simon a sharp glance, then a short nod as if unsurprised to see everyone gathered around a table where sat the six missing shoeboxes Devon and I had tried to find.

The Taos police must have released the four they'd been processing after they'd found them in Ginger La Ponte's house when they'd suspected her of her husband's murder, but I had no idea where the other two came from. From the glance Devon had given Simon, I figured the FBI agent had something to do with retrieving the four, so maybe he had also found the other two. Also, as none of the boxes were sealed, it stood to reason he knew all their contents—and if Simon knew, so did Devon.

From the looks the ladies shared, they realized that too. My mother leaned in as if to take one of the boxes, then seemed to change her mind. "Can we keep them?" she asked, her voice subdued.

Simon nodded, and a collective sigh came from the posse.

Mom smiled. "Well, this is certainly a big occasion. Not only is it Devon's thirty-first birthday, but thanks to his quick wit and handsome partner, he brought our boxes home."

"So, are you going to open them?" I asked.

"Oh, no. Not yet," Matilda said.

"Don't you think that's a bit unfair?" Babs asked. "After all, Devon and Simon went to so much trouble to get them back. Can't we know what's in them?"

"All in good time," Prudence said.

I shook my head, frustrated. After more than a year of searching for them and believing they held secrets that could possibly ruin the ladies' lives, I wanted to know what was in them. I almost strode over to grab them and tip the contents on the table, but I restrained myself. Just. Instead, I eyed Devon. He knew what the boxes held, and I was sure I'd be able to find out from him later.

"Well, that kind of ruins everything for tonight," Hilda announced. "I think we should all play charades."

"I have an idea," Trey said. "Why don't you tell me the story behind the boxes? Matilda has told me some of it, but I'd like to hear everything from the beginning."

"Oh, Trey, I did tell you. That's why Devon came home," Matilda said.

"Yes, you told me they went missing, but I imagine there's much more to all this. Humor me, Tillie, if you would."

I shook my head. I did not want a narrative of how the boxes went missing because I still felt a little guilty over my part in that disaster, though I'd never admitted my involvement to anyone. I glanced at Devon, hoping he'd intervene, but he simply smiled as if he also wanted to hear the tale.

Matilda nodded. "Well, all right, but as the boxes were at Kate's house, I think she should start."

Mom stood by the boxes and, after a dramatic pause to capture her audience, inclined her head. "It all began last spring when Colin and I decided to make a pilgrimage to Boston to discover our roots."

"Wait, what?" Babs shouted. "Boston? You were at the cabin."

"Don't be silly, dear. Why would we make a pilgrimage to the cabin?"

"I might suggest we all need a drink to sedate the audience," Prudence said, laughing.

As Marcy hopped up to pour out glasses of the champagne I'd had on ice, Babs leaned over to me with fire in her eyes.

"How can you calmly sit there knowing they played us."

At her indignation, I almost smiled, but unless we stormed out, which wouldn't go down well, we were stuck. "They told a little white lie. Come on, Babs. Aren't you a little curious about what's in the boxes?"

"Of course, dingdong," Babs said in a huff. She hadn't called me that in years, which only proved she was in a snit.

"Then let's hear her out, and we might learn something. *Then* we can plan our revenge. Deal?" I patted her leg, making her jump.

"Cut it out, Pip. I'll listen, but then she's going to hear from me."

Since I enjoyed seeing my mother and her favorite daughter at odds with each other, I decided to relax and watch the drama play out.

Marcy went around the circle handing everyone their flute of bubbly, then took her seat next to Hope.

"Well now, shall we continue?" my mom asked. "While Colin and I were in Boston, lovely city, by the way. If you've never been, you must head over to Marblehead. There's a woman there who makes fabulous pendants. Made from seashells. They are wonderful. Toria Marie. Look her up."

My mom fingered the pendant around her neck, which I had just noticed. It *was* pretty fabulous. "Are you wearing one now?"

"Oh yes, she made it with, of all things, squid ink. It's called Mystical Midnight."

"It's actually quite lovely," Babs admitted.

"It is. Anyway, while we were gone, the girls decided I was a hoarder and held a yard sale. Cleaned me out of house and home. And these boxes? These very special boxes? Yes, they sold them too."

I highly objected to her blaming *both* of us as it was Babs's idea. Babs organized it. Babs took care of the whole thing. Not me.

Devon squeezed my hand and leaned close to my ear. "Easy, Red."

"May I, Kate?" Matilda smiled as if retelling their tale was fun. "Well, once we discovered the boxes were gone, we took matters into our own hands. No sense in panicking."

"Mom, you called me and said it was an emergency and had me take the next flight home from Virginia. I'm not sure you can say you didn't panic," Devon remarked.

"And he dragged me along," Simon said.

"Wait, what?" As far as I knew, Devon had come home alone. He squeezed my hand again, but I glared at him, not mollified in the least.

"May I continue?" Matilda asked. "Now then. Devon arrived home, and we all went in search of the boxes. We did not find them though. We were distracted by other crimes and misdemeanors going on in Luckland."

Everyone nodded except Trey, who looked expectantly at Matilda. "Such as?" he asked, prompting her to continue.

"Some thugs stalked Pippa and violated her house," Hope said.

God, they were all getting in on the story. "She means I received a postcard with a written threat, then the Panello brothers broke into my house and trashed it. They stole my laptop and my camera."

"Oh, I'm so sorry, Pippa, that's awful," Trey said.

"Then we were all held at gunpoint when the Vegas thieves demanded the money back," my mom stated, taking back a little of the limelight.

"Mom!"

Though Devon already knew about the Vegas bag of millions, the ladies didn't know he knew. Devon and I had found a picture of Hope and Prudence with the carpetbag of cash and a newspaper clipping about a Vegas heist. At first, we'd thought they'd stolen the money, but when the posse had told Babs and me they'd found the bag of cash, I told Devon the truth so he wouldn't think his mother was a thief. Since then, we'd pretended Devon knew nothing about the money.

My mother waved her hand, dismissing my outburst. "Oh, pishposh, Pippa. I'm sure you've told him by now. Couples shouldn't keep secrets, you know."

From that, I assumed Trey also knew why Matilda had left Vegas in such a hurry after their whirlwind tryst all those years ago. I'd wondered what she'd told him. Now I knew.

"Devon saved us. He had his FBI team in place," Matilda said with a grin.

"Then you continued to look for the boxes?" Trey asked.

"Not exactly. We kept looking, but then Devon became Luckland's chief of police and had other duties to fulfill," Prudence said.

I bit back a retort at the fact the ladies kept saying "we." There was no "we" other than Devon and me looking for those boxes—and Simon, apparently.

"Unfortunately, when Prudence thought the aliens had returned, he had to investigate that," Hope said.

"Hold on a second," Martin said with a shake of his head.

"Let's keep this real. Someone blew up Prudence's basement, and we were investigating that. You lot were looking for aliens."

"As I'm sure I've told you," Matilda said. "Prudence married Professor Steppenhoffer, who drove her crazy thinking there were aliens on Earth."

"Who was arrested. The dirtbag is in jail," Martin said.

"Along with his son. Dirtbag number two," Dani announced. "While Jonathan terrorized Prudence, his son terrorized me."

"Then after we'd sorted all that, we got distracted again by the goon you knocked off in Tucson," my mom said.

"It was an accident," Trey said. "I didn't knock him off. However, that altercation did allow Matilda and me reunite." He placed an arm around her shoulders and brought her closer to him, adoration in his eyes.

"You know the rest," I said. "Hunter and Morgan pulled their haunted house stunt at the Manor. Then Monte murdered Henri La Ponte because of the recipes La Ponte stole from Hope and Marcy."

"And all of that happened because Babs sold the shoeboxes?" Trey asked.

"Actually, the shoeboxes had nothing to do with any of what happened," Prudence said. "Belle was behind the threats, unless…" She frowned. "Where did the other two shoeboxes come from?"

"I found them in Lois's house," Martin said.

I couldn't help my gasp, and I twisted to look at him. "*She* had them?" I remembered when Martin appeared with the boxes of letters, and he'd taken Devon out back to talk to him. That must have been when Martin told Devon about the shoeboxes. Why hadn't Devon told me? I turned to look at my boyfriend and scowled.

He shrugged. "I wanted to sur— Um, I wanted to give all

the boxes to the ladies at the same time. I knew the Taos police were ready to release the ones they had, so we kept the two Martin found until we got the other four back."

He'd been about to say he wanted to surprise me. He was lucky he hadn't managed to get that word out, though he'd still to get an earful when we were alone.

My mom's face tightened in anger. Like me, I assumed she was angry at Devon and Martin for not admitting Lois had two of the boxes. "The bitch could have given them back," she said. Oh, Mom was angry at Lois. That made sense too.

"She probably thought they held secrets she could use against us," Hope said, her tone bitter.

I waited to see if they'd say any more about the boxes' contents, but from the looks on their faces, that wasn't going to happen.

"What about the letters?" Prudence asked. "When can we get to read those?"

Devon and Simon shared a glance that spoke volumes. Devon sighed. "Not yet."

CHAPTER THIRTY

THE FOLLOWING MORNING, AFTER UNSUCCESSFULLY TRYING TO FIND out what the boxes held from Devon, I headed to the shop to do inventory. A small shipment had turned up, and I needed to photograph the items and get them on the website—and keeping busy was better than getting upset that my boyfriend was keeping a secret from me, especially as we'd agreed not to keep secrets from each other when it came to the ladies' antics.

As soon as I entered the back door, the little bells tinkling, I spotted my dad. I gave him a hug, needing the contact. When I let him go, I smiled, though I didn't feel any happier. "So, what came in?" I asked, forcing a light tone.

"Oh, there wasn't much, but I'm in the middle of refurbishing a set of dining chairs, and I need to focus on those."

I nodded. "That's fine. Call out if you need any help."

He wouldn't because I certainly wouldn't be able to help him. A magician when it came to restoration, my dad could transform anything from old and worn to profitable, and while I was creative, I wasn't good with tools. As my dad headed back to his workshop, I set up on a little desk and opened Roadrunner—my laptop I'd bought to replace the one the Panellos had stolen when they broke into my house, though they'd never admitted to it.

The small chest of goodies didn't take long to catalog, so I spent a bit of time making sure the inventory we had left matched that in the shop's stock database. After the Founders' Day influx of tourists, which was always a good revenue for Luckland's businesses, we had practically sold everything. My mom's job was to source and purchase new stock, which she mainly procured from auctioned estate sales, and from the almost empty store, she'd need to get some new items fast.

A couple of hours later, I stood at the shelves where Mom had displayed the last of Nadia McConnell's remaining pieces. My mom had purchased the estate in two lots, and all that was left were some books and a few porcelain knickknacks. There should have been a bejeweled box. I specifically remembered cataloging it, but it wasn't there, and according to the files, it hadn't been sold. With a frown, I headed over to my dad.

"What is it punkin?"

"There's a jeweled box missing. It was part of Nadia's estate. Do you think someone stole it?"

"Oh. Perhaps you should check with your mom."

There was an underlying hint in my dad's words that meant I should ask my mother if she had the box. I sighed. After Babs had cleared Mom's house, we'd hoped she'd stop bringing stuff home with her and cluttering her place up again. The accumulated clutter was the reason my mom and dad told Babs and me why they couldn't live together when the truth had nothing to do with clutter and everything to do with keeping Luckland's gold a secret. I understood the need for secrecy to some degree, but couldn't they have told Babs and me the truth?

Once I'd finished at the shop, I drove over to my mom's house. Oddly, I hoped the box *was* there. Otherwise, I would have to write it off as stolen.

My mom answered the door. "Pippa? Is everything all right?"

"I'm just checking on an item that might have ended up here," I said as I strode past her and headed to the living room. "Do you have a small, jeweled box about the size of a book from Nadia's estate?"

I realized I sounded abrupt, and with an internal sigh, I tacked on a smile. I'd already accepted I wouldn't get a truthful answer if I asked the women about the shoeboxes. Even Devon wouldn't tell me. So, if they wanted to keep their secrets, they could. I guessed I'd spent so much time looking for the shoeboxes and trying to help the ladies with their ongoing disasters, I felt an underlying disappointment they couldn't trust me enough with the truth.

"Oh. I do, actually." She quickly sped off. A few minutes later, she came back with a small box in her hands. "I'd almost forgotten about it. I'd intended to open it, but after that wretched chef died, it slipped my mind." She set the box on the coffee table and eyed the lock, which looked bent as if someone had tried to pry it open at one point.

I didn't remember the box having a damaged lock. "Was the lock like that when you brought it home?" I asked her as I picked up the box to examine it.

"Funny thing, now I think about it. I caught Hunter Jackson taking a look at it. When I went over to enquire if he wanted to purchase it, he dropped it and ran from the store."

"Hunter was interested in the box?" That didn't bode well. Anything to do with Hunter, Belle, and Nadia had the hairs on the back of my neck standing on end. That was when I remembered the little silver box with an image of Elroy inside the lid that I found in the shop last year. Belle had said Jonathan had bought it, but I'd believed it too much of a coincidence that the box had turned up just as we'd found the little alien statue. If

Hunter had been in the shop, it wasn't much of a stretch to imagine he'd left the box there for us to find. Well, at least that solved *that* mystery.

I gently tugged at the lock. The lid opened, and I peered inside.

"It's a diary," I said without thinking. The leather-bound journal was a few inches thick, and small, precise handwriting filled each page. I flipped through it. A few minutes later, I looked up.

"Oh my god. Call the posse," I said to her.

"The what?" My mother looked shocked.

"Call the ladies?" I hazard a guess my face looked sheepish.

"You and I need to talk," she said as she pulled out her phone and texted furiously.

CHAPTER THIRTY-ONE

December 23, 1959

It's been over ten years, but I remember that day so well. I woke up to find Momma was gone. I heard them fight again the night before. Then, in the morning, I went down to breakfast, and her place wasn't even set. Daddy ate with me. He never ate with me. He said Momma left on a trip. She never returned. I do recall hearing Andrew whispering in the storeroom. I am quite sure he knows something. I will ask later.

I looked up from the diary and assessed everyone's rapt attention

"Shall I go on?" I knew my mom was itching to grab the book from me, but it wasn't going to happen. While we'd waited for everyone to arrive, I'd already read through the diary and jotted down the pages to read.

February 14, 1960

Well, things are surely terrible now. Christmas Eve, I asked Andrew what he was whispering that fateful night to the house-keeper. Andrew said he had been over helping in the garden and heard my father call my mother a whore. I got so angry I slapped Andrew across the face, then burst into tears. Andrew was sweet and kind, and he looked at me in such a way my heart practically burst. He was so handsome that I did it. I kissed him. I'd always wanted to, but I was too young. I'm not anymore. I'm not too young at all. In fact, he kissed me back. We did more than kiss that night though.

This morning, Adelia found me in the bathroom with my head in the toilet. She knows. I pleaded with her not to tell my father. I begged her not to. He's never around anyway. He doesn't need to know.

No one moved. No one spoke. I had their undivided attention.

September 15, 1960

I didn't get to see her. They snatched her away. Just like that. Adelia and Carlo are gone too. They're all gone. They took her and left. Adelia told me she'd write and send pictures, and I managed to give her a box with an heirloom given to me by my grandfather.

"September fifteenth?" Hope whispered, clutching Marcy's hand tightly.

"Yes," I replied, holding her gaze. I could see the mix of emotions cross her face. Joy, fear, trepidation.

"Go on, Pip," Marcy said, placing an arm about Hope and bringing her close.

January 17, 1961

I got a letter today from Adelia. With a photo of Hope. That's her name. Hope. It's lovely. They had her bundled up as it snows there. Wherever there is. Nobody will tell me.

So, that was the confirmation Hope needed to know she was Nadia's daughter. She'd already told me she suspected her mother was Nadia or perhaps another illegitimate child of the McConnell line. I held up a hand and hurried to continue before the room erupted in chaotic chatter.

July 9, 1965

I got a letter from Adelia today. A picture of Hope all dressed up for Founders' Day. Whatever that might be. Hope looked like a little angel with her dark eyes and dark hair. All from Andrew, I imagine. I've not heard from him since that night. I do not know what became of him. I often wonder.

"There's one more entry, everyone, and I think this one may be the most important," I said.

May 20, 1972

I finally found out what happened to Momma. It's been so long, I hardly remember her, but after I asked Dad to please tell me, he agreed. He said she'd begun taking drawing classes to help her relax. She was, he said, a very high-maintenance woman. I do remember her being a bit excitable. He said she fell in love with her instructor and became pregnant. Mom and Dad had not been together as he'd been traveling, so he knew it wasn't his child. He did not want the rumor mill to get wind of it, so he sent her away to have the baby. It was all very discreet. She went to a private sanctuary in New Mexico.

The hard and sad truth was that she died there giving birth. The facility called him, and he went to see the baby, Mattie. He said he couldn't bring her home because he couldn't care for her, so he paid for a family there to care for her. They never formally adopted her though. He said she is still there, all grown up, and is doing well. He prefers I don't reach out, but if I must, he gave me her information. She goes by the name Belle Chantelle. He also said he spends time with her when he's there, taking care of his UFO society business. He said she works for him.

I am thinking of writing to her.

Well, that explained the mystery of why I hadn't been able to find anything about Nadia's mother when Mom had purchased Nadia's deceased estate.

My mom smiled. "Hope, that's so lovely to know for certain you're Nadia's daughter."

"Thank you, Kate, but it seems we've gotten things wrong. We all assumed Belle was Winston McConnell II's illegitimate daughter, but she wasn't. Do you think Nadia reached out to Belle? Does Belle know she's not a McConnell?"

"From Belle's obsession with being a Lucklander, I highly doubt it," I said.

Hope sighed. "I wonder if Andrew is still out there somewhere. After Mom and Dad died, I looked to see if I could find my biological parents, but the adoption was closed, and I got nowhere. I only found out I was a true Lucklander when—"

I tilted my head. "When what, Hope?"

"Why don't we all do DNA tests," Matilda said. "They're a great way to find out if we have other family members floating around the globe. You never know, Hope, you might find your biological father or some half sisters and brothers."

I suspected Matilda's idea was a way to distract me from asking Hope more questions, which meant the women had another secret they wanted to keep. I bit my tongue and decided if they didn't want to tell me, I wouldn't ask. I was fed up with their secrets and lies, and to be honest, I just didn't care anymore.

"On it," Dani murmured as she scrolled on her phone. "How many kits?"

Rosa stood and began counting heads.

"Don't forget the boys," Prudence said.

"Hilda, do you want to join in?" Marcy asked.

Hilda shook her head and looked about the room. "I have all the family I want or need right here."

CHAPTER THIRTY-TWO

"Oh, for flying lizard's sake, Mama, just spit." Dani held the tube in front of her mother's mouth, tapping a foot in frustration.

"Dani, if you do it, I don't see why I need to."

"Because with all these baby mommas without papas, we need to ensure we all know who we are. *Not* that I doubt you and Papa for a second." She rolled her eyes and smirked. The Valdez family was nothing if not affectionate. And PDA for Rosa and Pedro was commonplace.

Devon and Simon double-checked spit volume and sealed up the samples while Dani played spit collector. Martin was the only one not present as he was on duty, but he'd done his test earlier.

It had been a week since the reading of the infamous diary, and while we'd all waited for the test kits to arrive, we'd managed to reschedule the theater's grand opening for my mom's big show. The plan was to head over there after our spit session and get things ready. Hilda had somehow commandeered the role of choreographer from Matilda. I was staying out of that one. They needed to work together, and I wanted no part in it. My role was to photograph and video the big event.

Martin arrived unexpectedly and immediately headed to Devon.

"Just came from Louise Thorpe's," Martin said as he removed his hat and ran his fingers through his neatly trimmed salt and pepper hair. "Seems Lois had a visitor the day she died."

"Ha! I knew she'd bought stuff from that store because she was expecting company," my mom said.

"Who?" Prudence asked Martin.

"Louise said it was her sister's pen pal, Mattie, who we know is Belle. Louise said they were drinking tea and chatting."

"That's not right," Matilda said. "Lois detested tea. Never drank the stuff."

Martin frowned. "You don't say. Perhaps Louise just thought it was tea."

"Louise would know Lois hates tea, so why would Louise tell you she saw Lois drinking tea? That doesn't make sense," Prudence said.

I thought about that for a moment. "Prudence has a valid point. Plus, I seem to recall one of the letters making mention of Louise and Lois having a spat. I didn't think much of it, but shouldn't we go back and revisit?"

"Pippa is right," Devon said, abruptly standing. "It needs another look. I'll catch up with you all later." With that, he strode out, quickly followed by Simon. Martin also left, but at least he had the good grace to nod at us as he headed out the door.

"Curiouser and curiouser," I murmured. Something wasn't right. The fact that Belle saw Lois on the day she died set off alarm bells. "Marcy, I don't suppose you have your Tarot cards with you?"

The look the ladies gave me would have made me laugh if I hadn't felt it necessary to find answers. If Belle was involved, intuition told me Lois didn't die a natural death.

Marcy brought out the Tarot cards, and we all took our places on the floor. Babs had conveniently disappeared. She'd mentioned something about Leah and a playdate, but I was quite sure *she* was the playdate. Trey and my dad also excused themselves, which left my mom, Matilda, Prudence, Hope, Marcy, Hilda, Rosa, Dani, and myself.

"Okay, Luckland Ladies Posse, let's get this done." Prudence plopped down next to me.

"Wait, wait, wait. Since when do you call yourselves a posse?" That was my nickname for them, not theirs.

"Well, we've all taken a liking to it. So, there you are," Matilda said.

"Yes, but I'm not a member of your posse."

Silence. Not a good sign.

"Pippa, dear. Of course you are. You *and* Dani. Babs too, when she decides to show up."

"Do we not get to decide?"

Hilda laughed. "Oh, girl, you've got so much to learn. Now let's play cards."

I waited for Marcy to chide Hilda and remind her Tarot wasn't a game, but with Hilda being the eldest troublemaker, I assumed Marcy let it slide.

"How can we solve Lois's murder?" Marcy asked after cutting the deck and placing her hand over it. She then dealt out her cards in a pattern I hadn't seen before. She studied them intently, then nodded and looked up, sending her gaze around the circle.

"We're being deceived and misled. It's quite fascinating. There is an illusion to all that's happening, one we are prone to sink into. All is not as it seems, nor is it contrary. What confuses us most will be the truth of it all."

Hilda shook her head. "Girl, I love ya, but even that's more than I can understand. Translate that."

"Sorry, but you see here, the Moon, and over here, the Priestess. All of this is evidence that someone is playing us like a violin. We know the answer is not as simple as it seems, but whoever is behind Lois's death wants us to believe we have it all figured out. The Priestess tells us there is more. Something hidden we need to find. Over here is the Hermit. This tells us to look within ourselves and find the answers. There's one more secret we have yet to uncover that will break the illusion and lead us to the answers we seek."

"So, to paraphrase, Belle was the mastermind behind your threats, haunting the Manor, and stealing the cars, and even though she's behind bars, she's not finished with us yet. The cards are telling us to look a little deeper because there's one more secret that could help us find out how Lois died. How am I doing?" I asked, turning to Marcy.

"That's it. Yes."

"Well, then, who's up for a séance?" Hope asked.

"Hope, really? I think it's more down to using our brains now, not our psychic guides. Unless you can get Lali up here." I had a thought running through my head I needed to explore, and a séance wasn't going to help. "Give Dani and me a few hours. I have a hunch we can figure it out."

Dani smirked at me. "You do? We can?"

I stood, then reached down to pull her up with me. "Let's go, Dani girl. Time to kick some investigative ass."

CHAPTER THIRTY-THREE

I took a deep breath and tightly clenched Dani's hand. Then I knocked. A very polite three-rap knock. A friendly neighbor knock. Certainly not the knock of someone demanding answers.

The door opened, and I put my neighborly smile on.

"Pippa? Dani? Is there something I can help you with?"

I smiled a little brighter. "Oh, Louise. We just wanted to come by and bring over this casserole from the café and see if you needed some company. I know how hard things have been for you."

I thought I sounded quite convincing.

"Well, come in, girls, come in." She seemed welcoming, and I hoped this would be an easy conversation.

We entered the small but tidy home, and I immediately noticed that Louise had a green thumb. There were plants everywhere—not the silk flowers I tended to gravitate toward, mostly for the survival of plants everywhere, but beautiful flourishing ones. Dani stopped at a striking, pink flowering shrub in the hall. Louise quickly steered her away.

"No, no, Dani. Oleander is toxic. No touching."

Dani smiled sheepishly and shrugged as we followed Louise into the kitchen. I set the casserole down on her counter, then Dani and I sat at the kitchen table. It was a bit presumptuous, but we needed to be.

"So, how are you holding up, Louise? It must be so difficult for you," I said as she sat down.

"You don't know the half of it. Lois was all I had. We didn't always get along, especially when we were young, but over the years, we've grown quite close."

"I know. Babs and I are the same way. I hope someday we'll be as close as you two were."

"Well, you know, it just isn't fair. It's all Mattie's fault. She's the one who should be six feet under."

Mattie? So, did Louise not know the name Belle used now? Probably not. Lois may not have known.

Dani and I let Louise's comment slide because grief made a person say the most unusual things. It did make me wonder what she meant though. Why would Louise think Lois's death was Belle's fault, and why did Louise think Belle should be the one who died?

"So, will you be selling her house then?" Dani asked. "I noticed the For Sale sign in the yard."

I had missed that. Lois had lived next door to Louise. I needed to up my game.

"Oh yes, I've already called Letisha, and she put together a listing. I don't want to waste any time. As soon as I can, I'll have everything moved over here to the basement and go through it. She didn't have much, you know. I'll just keep the sentimental things, then have a yard sale."

"Well, if there's anything we can help you with, we'd be happy to, you know that."

"You know, there is one thing. Tell that bitch that Karma is gonna get her."

I'd not heard Louise curse before. "You mean Mattie?" I asked. "Why?" Did Louise suspect Mattie of murdering Lois?

A sudden knock on the door had us jumping.

"Oh, that's probably Devon. I told him we were stopping by." I'd just told a lie. I had no idea why he was here, but I knew that knock well.

A flush stained Louise's face as she stood. I glanced at Dani, who had begun scrolling away on her phone the moment Louise was out of sight. I waited for Dani to look up, and when she did, I raised a brow in question. She silently indicated I should check my phone just as it buzzed with a message.

Oleander poisoning. Often mistaken for natural causes of death. Can take hours to fully impact the system. Depending on dosage, it's lethal.

"You don't think..." I slammed a hand over my mouth as I suddenly realized what Dani was telling me. Louise had poisoned Lois.

Louise returned to the kitchen, bringing a smiling Devon and Simon. Even Louise had a smile on her face. Not for long.

"Come, boys, have a seat. Who's up for a glass of tea?"

Devon and Simon nodded.

Louise reached into the cupboard and pulled down several cups before she turned on the kettle. When Louise said a glass of tea, I thought she'd meant iced tea. Suddenly, I had the oddest sensation I'd seen this scene in a horror movie. Sweet old lady pouring tea, a drop of lemon, a drop of honey, and a smidge of arsenic. My breath caught in my throat. I looked at Dani. Then I glanced at the oleander.

I had one chance to tell Devon my theory without alerting Louise. I looked at Devon and smiled as naturally as I could, though by his expression, he saw right through my artifice.

"Say, Devon, sweetheart"—I never called him sweetheart—

"did you notice all the beautiful plants? Louise clearly has a green thumb."

"Can't say I noticed. You know I'm not much of a nature guy."

"Yes, but you must have seen the gorgeous pink flowers on the way in. What did you say those were, Louise?"

The kettle began to whistle, and she answered as she began to pour. "Oleander." She picked up the teacups, then placed one in front of Devon, then Simon. Odd that she hadn't offered Dani or me a drink.

I turned my phone screen toward Devon so he could see the message Dani had sent. Before Devon could say anything, Simon reached for the cup, causing Dani to suddenly jump up as if stung by a bee, her arm flying out and knocking the teacup clear off the table. Simon flinched.

"I am so sorry, Ms. Louise," Simon said, his southern creole accent heavy. He looked at Dani, bewildered. Louise quickly went to work, mopping up the mess.

"Oh no, you allow me to do that, Louise," Devon said, his tone calm as he held out his hand for a paper towel. While he wiped off the table, Louise took everything back to the kitchen bench. After discreetly tucking a piece of paper towel in his pocket, Devon slapped Simon on the shoulder.

"Seems there's a distress call out by the Manor. Maybe we should leave Louise while we go check it out. Girls?" Devon held out a hand for me to take, and we all quickly beat it out of Louise's house.

As we got to the curb, I yanked Devon's hand.

"Aren't you going to arrest her?"

"Well, I need a reason to, Pip. Right now, we don't know if Lois was poisoned. I told you the coroner took a blood sample, but he hasn't come back to me with a report. When he does, and if it's positive for poison, I'll come back with a warrant. I promise.

"She was going to poison you too," I whispered as if saying it quietly wouldn't hurt as much.

Simon and Dani had walked ahead, and both looked mad as wasps. Knowing Dani, she didn't explain her actions, and Devon hadn't had a chance to either. Simon probably thought Dani had lost her mind.

CHAPTER THIRTY-FOUR

"Son of a bitch!"

I heard Devon's shout from all the way out back as I gave Billy and Skye a few bedtime hugs and fed them. Even their ears perked up. Devon wasn't big on swearing out loud. Even less on yelling. Something wasn't right, and I immediately headed inside.

I found him in the kitchen, strapping on his weapon. Never a good sign when he was off duty.

"What happened? You look madder than a rattler."

"No time for fun and games, Pip. Those women have done it again."

"I'll bite. What did they do this time?"

"Might as well come along for the ride. Dani and Simon are already out front." He shook his head. Whatever happened must have been monumental.

In my polka dot pj's and bunny slippers, I wasn't really dressed for adventure, but I was certainly not going to stay home. I followed him out the door, but he suddenly stopped and gave me a top to bottom look.

"What the hell are you dressed as?" He smiled even through his annoyance at the ladies.

"Don't worry about what I'm wearing. Lead the way, and let's go head off that impending disaster."

Dani and Simon were already in Simon's SUV, so Devon and I got into his patrol car, and they followed us.

"Where are we headed? Where's the emergency?" I asked, buckling up before he reminded me. I had no idea where we were headed, but I anticipated lights, sirens, and some decent speed to get there.

"You'll see." He clenched his jaw. Whatever the disaster, it was big. We traveled fast, but no lights or sirens. I nervously tapped my fingers on the armrest. I had no idea what the posse could have done, but as we slowed and turned onto Louise Thorpe's street, I had an inkling.

Matilda's SUV sat outside Louise's house, and all the ladies had gathered in a circle on the sidewalk.

"Want to clue me in now, Kemosabe?" I asked as we parked.

Devon grumbled something and exited the car. I hurried to catch up as Devon strode over to the barely visible women in their traditional nighttime stealth garb of black leggings and leotards. We'd only seen them thanks to Devon's headlights. Thankfully, Devon left them on so we could at least see the group of mischief-makers.

Dani and Simon arrived and parked behind us. Dani quickly came up next to me.

"What's the scoop?" she asked.

"No clue."

We cautiously approached the circle and waited to hear what Devon had to say.

"What the hell are you all doing?" he asked, loud and commanding.

I bit back a grin. He'd broken the first rule—always direct the question to *one* of the women, never all.

"Citizens' arrest, Devon," Hilda said.

I peered around Devon. The women had Louise trapped in their center.

"She did it, you know. It was Louise the whole time," said Matilda.

"Chief Marks, I demand you have them release me." Louise sounded perturbed.

Devon closed his eyes and tilted his face to the heavens. That was what he did when exasperated.

"We caught her trying to leave town," Hope said. "Why else would she leave town?"

"That's right," Rosa said. "She was hightailing it."

"Do you have evidence of a crime?" Devon was clearly not bringing his A game.

"Of course we do," my mother replied. "She murdered her sister."

"In cold blood," said Prudence.

"It was the tea leaves," said Hope.

"*La adelfa es veneno, ya sabes*," Rosa said.

"The oleander is poison," Dani whispered to me, translating.

"All right, ladies. I'm going to need you to back away for a moment. Please." Devon stepped forward and nudged Matilda first.

The other women all took a step back, but just one—as if afraid Louise would escape. Devon took a few steps into the circle.

"Thank heaven you've arrived," Louise said, her tone nasty for someone being rescued.

"I'm going to need you to turn around with your hands behind your back, Louise. You're under arrest."

Now that was a stunner. Everyone gasped, including me. Devon had said he'd need proof before he could act. So, did that mean he had it?

"For what, young man? You can't believe I'd murder my sister?" Visibly upset, tears flowed down her face as Devon cuffed her. Then Louise started to shriek as Devon read her rights, advising her not to say anything.

It didn't stop her.

"It wasn't my fault. She shouldn't have touched the cup. The tea was meant for Mattie. Mattie did it. Mattie convinced Lois to drink it."

What part of *you have the right to remain silent* didn't she understand? Not that I cared since she'd also tried to poison Devon and Simon.

"She promised us she'd find the gold, and we'd share it. Then that crazy bitch double-crossed us. Brought Hunter into it."

Devon sighed. "Louise, I'll need to remind you that everything you say can and will be used against you, so I suggest you stop talking now."

She glared at Devon but stopped her rant. I didn't think it mattered at that stage. She'd basically admitted she'd accidentally murdered Lois when attempting to murder Belle.

CHAPTER THIRTY-FIVE

"So, what has you all in a twist?" Devon asked the following morning as he served up coffee and some incredible cinnamon coffee cake.

When I'd come into the kitchen, he'd been humming, which possibly related to some secret he hadn't yet revealed about Louise the murderess. He'd been out late last night, hauling her off to jail.

I grinned. "Devon, the expression is *what has your panties in a twist.*"

"I am not saying that, ever." His still damp hair had curled around his neck, and as he laughed, his eyes sparkled. For some reason, the man was extra gorgeous in the morning—which might be because he often made me breakfast.

"Well, we've been invited to a thing," I said as I held up a card and envelope from the mail I'd picked up on the way to the kitchen.

"Here, let me see." Devon reached across the table to take the card.

Batting his hand away, I shook my head. "Not until I've read it to you. Have some patience."

You are cordially invited to attend the
Re-Grand Opening
of
Murphy's Playhouse
When: Saturday
Where: Murphy's Playhouse
Time: 7 P.M.
Unveiling to follow at The Cabin.

Devon grinned. "Well, that was quite expected, considering I've been over there every night helping rebuild the set."

"With my help," Simon said, coming into the kitchen to join us. Unannounced, as he tended to do.

"Well, hello, Simon. What plans have you today? Last I heard, you were headed out to scout for a place of your own?" I phrased my statement as a question, though it was more wishful thinking. He hadn't really overstayed his welcome, but I wasn't sure of his intentions. Dani had stayed just as long, but at least I knew she had somewhere to go at some point. Either she'd be off on a dive or down to see her folks in Arizona. Simon didn't seem to be headed anywhere.

"Now that you mention it, Pip, I may just be on the lookout for something. My lease in Denver is up soon."

I covered my mouth so he wouldn't see me smile. Simon moving to Luckland would surely spice things up for him and Dani. "I'll be happy to put my ears to the ground for you, Simon. I'm sure something will pop up."

"Of course, it will. Just mention it to the ladies, and they'll take care of it." Devon was only half kidding. He still smarted from the whole incident where the ladies bought us Mystic Manor before we'd declared ourselves a couple. He did have a point though. All Simon had to do was hint he might want to stay, flash those pearly whites, and the perfect house would just appear. Like magic.

"Take care of what?" Dani's asked from the stairs. She had to have been listening.

"Simon wants to live here," I announced with a grin.

"Here? As in this house? Seriously, Simon. Give these two a break, would you? Go find your own place." Dani shook her head and headed for the coffeemaker.

Simon tossed back his head, let out a rich, very sexy laugh, and winked at her, which caused her to nearly drop the mug in her hand.

"Now we've all assembled, maybe you boys could fill us in on how that whole arrest went down? It was, as you know, *our* idea that she was the guilty party," I said as Dani and I looked at them expectantly.

"Belle confessed, trying to cop a deal," Devon replied matter-of-factly. "She said she tried to get Lois to drink the tea after spotting Louise put something in it. Belle knew Lois hated tea, so she told her it had something to make her nighttime hot flashes go away."

"Belle killed Lois?" Dani asked.

Simon smiled. "Yes and no, chérie. Belle killed Lois, yes, but so did Louise. It's all about intent. Louise poisoned the tea that killed her sister. Therefore, she killed her sister."

I took a very deep sip of coffee, then sighed. "My head is spinning. Who gets charged with murder?"

"They both do," Devon and Simon answered simultaneously, then they fist bumped each other.

"So, the two of them are locked up, and life can go back to normal?" I asked, quite hopeful for a yes but somehow knowing there was more.

"As normal as can be expected," Devon replied with a grin.

Then he and Simon shared a look, which caused alarm bells to go off in my head. Apparently, they went off in Dani's head too.

"Spill it, guys. You have something up your sleeve, don't you?" Dani leaned into the table and locked her gaze on Simon's. "Out with it."

Devon and Simon shared another look, then Simon's whole face lit up. "I've decided to hang up my G-boots. Going rogue." Simon sat back and waited for a reaction.

"English, Simon," Dani said.

"I'm leaving the FBI and going into private practice. With Devon."

"Wait, you two are setting up your own agency? What kind of agency?" she asked.

"You tell 'em," Simon said to Devon.

"An investigative agency," Devon said.

I frowned. "I know you were going to start an investigation firm last year, but you changed your mind when the ladies organized the chief of police job."

Devon's lifted a brow. "They did *what*?"

Oops.

Tense silence filled the kitchen, then Devon laughed. "You had to realize I knew the ladies were behind the job."

"You knew?" That was news.

"Of course, I did, but I wanted to stay in Luckland, and that was the easiest way."

Warmth filled my chest as he'd wanted to stay in Luckland because of me. "So, you want to give up the chief of police position?"

"Pip, running the Luckland PD is not an overwhelming job. I have some extra time on my hands. Simon is tired of being a Fed, so starting an investigative firm is perfect."

As I fully supported him for going after his dream, I smiled.

"Until then, who's got the skinny on this *unveiling* at the cabin? What does that even mean?"

Sitting in the theater felt like déjà vu. An expectant hush took over the audience as my dad led my blindfolded mom down the aisle and into the front row. The anticipation grew. Only this time, my mother certainly knew what was about to happen.

The curtains rose, and the actors took their places on stage. Then for the next two hours, Dani, Simon, Devon, and I were totally enthralled as the women presented Hope's debut musical: Rock and Roll Road Trip. I wasn't sure what happened to the original play they were supposed to perform, Shade Song Lilies, but I didn't imagine it could have been any more fun.

While Hope had clearly changed the characters' names, they were based on all of us. Trey and Matilda starred in the leading roles. He as Jon Von Jobi, and Matilda as Tillie Temptation. The rest of the cast came from the high school drama club.

After spending the evening watching our personal dirty laundry and misadventures, all the women gathered on stage, apart from my mom. The lights turned down, and the spotlight focused on her in the front row. Matilda stepped forward, holding the mic.

"Kate Murphy O'Leary, welcome to Luckland's newest attraction, our new community theater."

Hope stepped forward and took the mic from Matilda. "Because, dear Kate, it has been your lifelong dream to be a part of the theater, we hereby dedicate this wonderful space, Murphy's Playhouse, to you."

Hope handed the mic to Prudence. "Our first official act, as trustees of this treasure, is to name our new director." Hope waved her arm toward my mom. "Kate Murphy O'Leary."

The entire audience, which was basically the entire town, stood and applauded while my mom simply burst into tears. Finally, she stood, and after slowly twirling around and taking it all in, she nodded. The ladies waved her forward, yelling for her to come join them.

She took her time making her way to the steps on the side, then slowly ascended to the stage and made what could only be described as a grand entrance. The one she'd waited her entire life to make.

While the ladies had a group tear and hug fest, the four of us slipped outside and headed home. The night wasn't over though. We had an *unveiling* to attend.

CHAPTER THIRTY-SIX

Arriving at the cabin always took my breath away, no matter how many times I'd been there. The entire home had three hundred and sixty-degree views from atop a mountain. Though rustic, it boasted six bedrooms and bathrooms, and a full gourmet kitchen. The interior lights flooded the front porch, leading us into the warmth and general buzz.

My curiosity had climbed to an all-time high on the drive up there. I was sure the ladies were finally going to tell us what was in the shoeboxes, and sure enough, the moment Devon, Simon, Dani, and I stepped into the large open space of the great room, we were greeted by the six boxes sitting on the mantel of the stone fireplace.

By Luckland standards, the gathering at the cabin was exclusive. Seated around the room were two generations of Lucklanders and their significant others. Well, three genera-tions if I counted Leah, which I did. When Simon received the same invite as the rest of us, there were two reasons why I thought the posse had included him. One, they might have already decided to classify him as Dani's significant other even though Dani still insisted nothing was going on between them.

Two, because he already knew what was in the boxes. Hilda was there, of course. As an honorary posse member, there was no way she'd miss any of this.

My mother stood in front of the fireplace.

"It's time," she said. "Our boxes have returned home, and it's time you all understood their importance."

"I think it's past time, Mother, don't you?" Babs asked, blurting out the obvious.

"Very well. Before we open them, there are things you need to know."

Babs blew out a breath. "Duh," she muttered.

"Moving on." My mom darted a pointed look at Babs. "Each of these boxes holds its own treasure, but only one holds the keys to the kingdom."

Here we go. Talk about melodramatic. I was excited though. We were finally going to learn the infamous shoeboxes' secrets.

"I will tell you what we were told all those years ago," my mother said. "The year we all turned thirty-one, we were brought up here to this sacred ground."

Sacred?

"Unfortunately, my parents and Hope's were no longer with us, so Matilda's and Prudence's parents sat us down and told us a story of luck and hardship. A story of determination. A story to be passed down. You know the story by now—about how our ancestors found Luckland and made it their home. They also found a treasure. Rich veins of gold that they carefully mined."

I frowned. Mom had told us the founders had sealed the mine, but apparently not before they took some of the gold. Devon must have noticed my expression because he reached over and took my hand. Probably as a warning not to interrupt. It was okay for him. Like Simon, he already knew what was in the boxes. I just wanted my mom to hurry up.

"We are all connected. Just as the earth is inextricably

linked to the sun, moon, and stars, so are we all linked as the sons and daughters of the universe."

When Hope, Prudence, Matilda, and Rosa stood and joined my mother in front of the mantel with the boxes, I half expected them to start chanting.

One by one, the women selected a box and, without fanfare, opened it. Each pulled out another box from within, and after placing their shoebox on the floor, carefully held the smaller box in front of them. There they stood, five women with five small wooden boxes. Each box had an intricately carved pattern on the top, though I couldn't see them clearly. I had to resist the urge to go over to examine them.

With a nod from my mom, they opened the wooden boxes and pulled out what appeared to be ancient-looking medallions. I couldn't tell for sure, but they appeared to be gold and attached to a gold chain.

Ginger had four of those boxes. No way was she uninterested in the contents, as she claimed. The gold must be worth a fortune, and the fact she and her now dead husband had come to Luckland *looking* for secret recipes and gold... She'd lied.

The women arranged the small boxes on the floor next to the shoeboxes. Then, as if they'd done this for decades, the women placed the medallions about their necks, stretched their hands above their heads, closed their eyes, and began to chant.

I almost rolled my eyes.

At first, they were so quiet I couldn't make out what they were saying. I squeezed Devon's hand to get his attention. He glanced at me and smiled softly, nodding toward them. His way of saying pay attention, I supposed.

That was when I remembered the women had said the contents of the boxes had to do with the spirits that would rise if anyone disturbed the sacred ground on which the founders had built Luckland. Yet Mom had also said *this* was sacred ground. So, were the medallions supposed to protect Luckland *and* the cabin against spirits? Were the women also supposed to do their annual Founders' Day ritual at the cabin but couldn't without the medallions? Was that why I had seen an apparition of an old man by the barn, and Devon had seen a ghostly child on the road near here?

Suddenly, everyone except Hope lowered their arms.

"*Gaoth an Tuaiscirt, tabhair le chéile muid, déan iomlán dúinn ionas go bhféadfaimis ár bhfortún a dhaingniú,*" Hope uttered, a slight lilt to her voice.

"Show off," Prudence muttered, scowling.

I had no idea what Hope said. I would have asked for a translation, but it didn't seem appropriate to interrupt their ceremony—not if it was going to appease Luckland's spirits.

Hope lowered her arms as Prudence raised hers. "Wind of the South, bring us together, make us whole that we may secure our fortune."

Then it was Matilda's turn. "Wind of the East, bring us together, make us whole that we may secure our fortune." Matilda stretched to her full height as if trying to reach the sky.

"*Viento del Oeste,*" Rosa intoned before grinning at Prudence. "Wind of the West, bring us together, make us whole that we may secure our fortune."

At least I'd figured out what Hope had said. I had no idea what language though. Maybe Gaelic, as their ancestors were Irish. There was a pause as they all raised their arms and grabbed one another's hands. I assumed they were tapping into the Native American magic they often spoke about.

That was when my mom spoke. "The four winds have gathered, and under the Sun, the Moon, and the Stars, we shall all be one," she said.

So, the women *were* the four winds. That was what Belle

had needed when she'd tried to get the goat house to open. Granted, she'd thought it was a gold mine.

Just then, I swore the earth shifted beneath my feet. The lights flickered, and the windows rattled, exactly like they had when the posse had done a séance at Mystic Manor last year, though this seemed different, more ominous. I squeezed Devon's hand. I needed his comfort and energy. Whatever the ladies were doing, it was just one step beyond creepy, which was saying a lot—and there was still one shoebox left to open.

CHAPTER THIRTY-SEVEN

MY MOTHER APPROACHED THE MANTEL AND RETRIEVED THE SIXTH shoebox before she placed it on the floor in the middle of the circle. Then backing up, she took her place alongside the women and gripped their hands again.

"The winds have gathered, and under the Sun, the Moon, and the Stars, we shall all be one." They all repeated the chant in unison, then retreated, leaving the box in the center of the room.

"Pip, Babs, Dani, Devon, please go stand around the box. In a circle, clasping hands," my mother said.

We exchanged a few nervous glances but rose and did as she asked. We encircled the shoebox, clasped hands, and waited for further instructions. The hair on the back of my neck wasn't just standing at attention; it was electrified.

"Repeat these words," my mother said quietly. "We are the sons and daughters of the wind. We stand before you, seeking the wisdom that will one day be ours."

After a moment's hesitation, we did her bidding.

"We are the sons and daughters of the wind. We stand before you, seeking the wisdom that will one day be ours."

"Pippa, open the box," my mom said, nodding toward it.

"Me? Why me?"

At her raised brow, I squatted next to the box and lifted off the lid.

I wasn't sure what I expected to find. Perhaps something like the women's medallions, an ancient scroll, or some bottles of magic potion. Instead, I saw folded bits of paper, some photos, a small booklet that could have been the recipes, and a thumb drive. Well, that was disappointing. I was about to reach for one of the pieces of paper when my mother's voice rang out, stopping me cold.

"No touching, Pip. It's Devon's turn."

I spared her a glance then retreated and sat back down. I might have stuck out my tongue at Devon, just for old times' sake. He smirked and stepped over to the box.

"Devon, the box holds the key. You'll need to find it."

There wasn't a key unless the papers and photos hid it. I'd surreptitiously peeked into the other five shoeboxes. All were empty, so I could only surmise each of the ladies had transferred their "secret treasures" into the sixth box. I assumed one of the pieces of paper was a copy of Devon's birth certificate. Therefore, one of the photos was probably the original of the one sent to Tony the Tiger to intimidate Trey. I still wasn't sure who had sent Tony after Trey. Even though Lois had two of the boxes, making threats was Belle's forte. However, the sisters and Belle had worked together to find the gold, so maybe they were all to blame.

Devon pulled out the thumb drive.

Matilda began clapping. "Well done. I knew I raised a bright boy."

"Babs, please replace the lid," my mother said as if her request wasn't at all strange.

"Don't I get a souvenir?" she asked. "How come Devon got to take something from the box?"

"No worries. You'll all be getting a souvenir," Prudence said with a laugh.

As Devon sat down beside me, I leaned into him. "I thought she told you to find a key. Why would you choose a thumb drive?"

"Because if you want to stash something, that's how you do it."

That made no sense at all. "Why didn't you tell me what was in the boxes?"

"They weren't my secrets to tell. Anyway, there wasn't anything in there we didn't already know about, except the thumb drive and the medallions. If I'd told you about them, what would you have done?"

"Ask them to explain why they were so important."

"Which is what they are doing now."

Trust him to be logical about it. "Will you promise me, no more secrets?"

He smiled. "I'll try."

I sighed. For a man who didn't like others to have secrets, he certainly had quite a few of his own.

After Babs closed the lid to the shoebox, my mom gathered all the boxes and placed them on the mantel. "All right, everyone, let's go."

"Where?" Babs jammed her hands on her hips. "This is getting to be weird, Mother. I mean, really, what are we doing?"

"Just follow along." Mom strode over to my dad and took his hand before they headed out the back door. We all followed, with Trey carrying Leah, for about a hundred yards until we ended in a small clearing surrounded by a thick copse of towering pine. In the middle, camouflaged by brush and twigs, was what appeared to be a pair of cellar doors with an old iron handle.

I shook my head. "What is this?"

"Patience, Pip," my father said, not unkindly.

He pulled on the handle and opened the doors. Dani, Simon, Babs, Tom, Devon, and I leaned in to see what lay beneath. Everyone else stood back as if they already knew what we'd find, including Martin and Trey. So, was this a younger generation thing?

I was the first to lean back. "It's pitch dark down there. What are we supposed to see?"

Devon produced a flashlight and winked. Seriously? Turning it on, he glanced at my dad for approval, which he gave. My dad let Devon have whatever Devon wanted. He shone the light at the empty void in the ground.

"You're kidding me, right?" I looked in and cringed. I wasn't one for dark, creepy places.

Babs shoved me aside with her hip and leaned over to look. "What is that? The ladder to hell?"

"It's here, isn't it?" Devon pointed to the hole in the ground. "That's where all the gold is."

"See? Brilliant," Matilda said. Her praise was actually becoming annoying. He wasn't the only one with a brain.

"When you invoked the four winds, which set off the rumbling, you were using the Native American magic that infuses the land around Luckland, and those medallions have something to do with it. You basically opened a gateway, didn't you?" I looked at my mother, who smiled like the cat who'd found the mouse.

"Excellent observation, Pippa."

I gave Devon a cheeky grin and winked. I could be brilliant too.

"Yadda, yadda, and all that," Hilda said. "Let's get this gold digging underway, shall we?"

"Aunt Hilda, may I remind you it's not our gold?" Marcy threw Hilda a death glare.

"Of course it is, Marce." Hope turned to Marcy and leaned up to give her a kiss. "You're mine, I'm yours, and all we have is ours."

God, they were the cutest couple.

"Well, if nobody else is going down, I will," Dani said as she stepped over to the built-in ladder. "This is like climbing down for a dive." She grinned. "In the dark."

"I think you might need help, chérie." Simon strode over and stood next to her.

"I'll take the lead," Devon announced.

I frowned. I didn't like the idea of him descending a ladder to nowhere.

Devon smiled, then kissed me. "Remember, I'll always have your back."

Well, I couldn't *really* say no to that.

He began the climb down, and I followed. Simon came next, followed by Dani. Then Tom and Babs. As I approached the bottom of the ladder, Devon grabbed me about the waist, swung me around, and planted me on the ground. Swoon-worthy really. He shone his flashlight around to get a grasp on our surroundings—which was how I spotted a light switch.

CHAPTER THIRTY-EIGHT

One flick of a switch bathed the chamber in light. Electric? Battery? I had no clue, but I was more interested in the door in the wall. A vault door. The kind you can't open without, it appeared, knowing how. No handle, no big wheel like in the movies, no keypad, nothing. Just a big steel door.

I looked at Devon, who studied it intently. Simon too. Babs stood next to me. Her face scrunched in confusion, mirroring mine.

"How the hell does it open?" Dani asked.

"My guess is it's either a remote system or code-based," Tom said quietly. "I've installed some of these in clients' homes. The paranoid ones."

Devon turned to Tom and grinned. "You do security work? We might need you on some of our jobs. Simon and I are going into business. We could always use a third."

I cleared my throat. "Um, the door?"

Tom stepped closer and began to feel around the frame of the metal door with his fingers. He suddenly stopped to look at Devon. "You have that thumb drive?"

Devon snuck a victorious look my way.

"That I do, Tom." He pulled the small device from his pocket and handed it to Tom, who quickly inserted it into what I assumed was an opening he'd found.

"It should be automatic. Takes a minute or two to read it, then we'll see," he said.

We all held our breath and stared at the door, waiting for something to happen. Then a small click sounded. We all glanced at one another, then waited some more. It was the longest minute of my life.

The door began to vibrate, then slowly opened, swinging away from us into the vast darkness beyond. When it was fully open, the six of us remained still. Personally, I wasn't ready to just barrel on in. Not without knowing what we'd encounter.

Another minute ticked by. The room began to lighten as if something had triggered a dimmer switch. Gradually, the contents of the vault became visible.

"Jesus, Mary, and Josephine," Babs said, crossing herself as if she were familiar with the religious rite.

"I believe there's gold in them thar hills." I almost giggled at my ridiculous statement because the vault was stacked high, floor to ceiling, with bars and bars of the shiny stuff.

Devon hesitantly shifted toward the door. He probably thought it was booby-trapped.

"I'm sure nothing will fall on your head, Dev. After all, your mother sent you down here." I hoped that would reassure him.

He turned and grinned at me. "That's what I'm afraid of."

I stepped up next to him and held his arm for good measure, and after staring at each other for a moment, we strode into the small room. When nothing exploded or attacked us, the others followed.

I wasn't an expert on gold and had no idea what the stacks

of gold bars, each the size of a candy bar, meant. "Dani, what are we looking at?"

"A treasure hunter's wet dream," she replied, deadpan.

Simon snickered, causing Dani to bite back a grin.

"If I'm not mistaken, and I rarely am, those are kilobars. Thousands of them." She surveyed the stacks in front of her, then glanced at the side walls, also stacked high. "If there are multiple layers beyond the wall face, we're looking at upward of half a billion dollars."

Bab's face turned ashen. Tom's expression wasn't much better. Dani shook her head. She'd been on more than her fair share of treasure dives, so for her to be in awe was a surprise. Simon appeared curious but not overwhelmed. Devon seemed horrified.

I grabbed his hand and squeezed, as he often did to me.

"What's going through your head, Dev?" I asked quietly— for his ears only.

He looked down at me, his eyes filled with worry. "How am I supposed to protect you now? You're an heiress."

I stood on my toes to give him a kiss. "And you, my love, are an heir."

None of us made a move to touch the gold. After a few minutes, we headed back through the vault door. Devon removed the thumb drive. The door closed by itself.

We climbed back up where everyone waited. With crickets the only sound, we stood on one side of the black hole and stared at the women and their partners on the other. Clearly, each side waited for the other side to break. Finally, I could bear it no longer.

"Someone has some explaining to do." I stared straight at my mother.

"You all look like you've just seen Marley's ghost," Hilda

said, coming over to stand with us. "You did take a picture of whatever hell on fire was down there? Didn't you?"

"Nope. We did not," I said.

Simon grinned. "Picture it, Hilda. A cabin in the woods. A big black hole. And a whole lotta gold."

Hilda grinned back. "You know, Simon, if I were twenty years younger…"

"Aunt Hilda, if you were twenty years younger, you'd still be older than dirt."

"Can we please get back to what lies beneath?" Babs impatiently tapped her foot.

"Very well, back to the cabin, everyone. It's story time." Hope began swiftly marching away.

My dad and Trey grabbed the cellar doors and shut them—though without a lock, I wasn't sure what that would do other than prevent someone from falling into the black hole.

Devon paced the living room floor. "How much gold is in there?"

"Well, we don't really know. We've never counted the bars. We only use up about, oh, a dozen a year." Matilda rotated her hand from side to side as she spoke.

"Wait, what do you mean 'use up'?" Devon stopped his pacing and stared at Matilda.

"We have a dealer who sells the bars to different buyers around the country." Matilda patted his shoulder, then headed off to pour herself a drink.

"You have no idea how many bars there are? Okay then, how much is a bar worth?" he demanded, still standing in the middle of the living room.

"Oh, that will vary. When gold is up? Maybe fifty-five thousand or so," Hope said.

"Per bar?" I asked.

"Why, of course," my mother said.

"Where did it come from? The mine?" Devon finally strode over to join me on the sofa.

Prudence nodded. "Well, yes, where else?"

"But it didn't come out of the mine that way," I said.

"Of for criminy sake, Pippa. Our founders dug up the ore and melted the gold into bars, which they then stored. Eventually, when they sealed the mine, they brought the gold up here." Prudence seemed a bit touchy, but after I thought about what I'd said, I didn't blame her.

"Why didn't they just store the bars at a depository?" Devon looked at my mom for an answer.

"Too many questions."

"So, that begs the question of proof of ownership," Simon said. "You do realize that gold bullion needs to be registered."

"Yes, but our ancestors didn't inform the government of the gold, and there's a reason for that," Hope said.

Simon narrowed his eyes. "Which is?"

Hope smiled. "Let me explain by telling you about our ritual. You saw what we did tonight, invoking the four winds. That was to ensure our and your safety."

"Against what?" I asked.

"The spirits of the dead, dear. When our founders arrived where Luckland now lies today, they brought with them two Native American wives whom they met on their voyage across the continent. The women realized the ground was a sacred burial site and urged our ancestors not to settle there or look for gold. Unfortunately, the men didn't listen. They found the gold and started digging."

"That's when the spirits began to haunt them," Prudence said, joining in on telling the story. "Accidents happened, and the hauntings grew worse. Curses were placed upon our ancestors' heads."

Babs, whose color had returned to normal, went nearly white as a sheet. "Curses? What curses?"

"We don't know exactly, but after realizing the errors of their ways, the men stopped digging and sealed the mine. But the souls of the dead continued to elicit nightmares and disturb the men's minds," Matilda said a little dramatically. She could have rivaled my mom in that department.

"Our great-great-great-grandmothers crafted an incantation to appease the spirits, and eventually, the specters stopped their hauntings. So, each year, on Founders' Day, we do the same incantation," my mom said.

Babs took a deep breath. "Your ritual."

"Yes."

"What about the medallions? What do they do?" I asked because I remembered the ladies' anxiety when they'd gone off to perform the ritual this year and last. They didn't have the medallions then.

"They're filled with magic. Blood magic. We need them for the ritual to work," Hope said. "And before you ask, if anyone other than a descendant tries to do the ritual with the medallions, nothing happens. They only work with descendants."

Because they have our ancestors' blood in them? I shivered.

"So, the ghosts we've seen around Luckland are because you didn't have the medallions?" Dani asked.

Hope nodded. "Basically, yes."

"That was why you were so desperate to get the boxes back," Devon said. "You should have told us, not that it would have helped us find them, I suppose, but still."

The crease between his eyes showed his annoyance. I didn't

blame him. The knowledge of the gold and the ritual should have been something they told us, not kept secret.

"So why did you tell us now?" he asked.

"You are all of age, and it's now your responsibility to carry the secret of the mine and the gold, and to perform the ritual," his mom answered.

"Oh, no. No way. I'm not going to stand in a circle and start calling on winds and stars and moons. Nope." Babs shook her head and looked ready to leave.

"I like the pretty, twinkling stars," Leah said.

"I know, sweetie, but Mommy doesn't want to break wind."

I laughed, and Dani grinned. The ladies, however, all frowned.

"The descendants of the four founders must carry on the tradition. It's imperative to save the residents of Luckland," my mom declared. "If more spirits rise and converge, all hell could break loose. Literally."

"So, you're saying the four of us are it?" Dani asked.

"Yes, it's your legacy. You are the keepers of Luckland," Prudence said, her face solemn.

Simon tapped his fingers on his knee. "To be clear, the founders sealed the mine and didn't tell the government about the gold because if word got out, others would quickly converge on the area and dig up the sacred ground to get to the gold, correct?"

Rosa smiled. "Exactly, Simon. The founders couldn't risk the lives of those in Luckland. So, instead of the ones destroying the Native American ground, they became its guardians."

"Is the gold cursed? Is that why you had to do that ritual to open the vault? I mean, we're miles from Luckland." I thought it a reasonable question, and by Devon's quick smile in my direction, he thought so too.

Hope shrugged. "We don't know. After a hundred and

seventy years, some explanations became lost, but we certainly aren't taking a risk. That rumble you felt happens every time we have to open the vault, so we thought it best to keep doing the incantation."

"May I have a closer look at your medallion, Mother?" Babs asked. My mom took hers off and handed it to Babs, who examined it closely, then handed it to me. The medallion was heavy, with a Celtic cross and several Native American symbols engraved on the front. On the back, it had the initials SM.

"SM?" I asked. "Sean Murphy?"

Mom nodded. "That's right. Each medallion was handed down to the firstborn in each family. However, we had one made for Rosa because Prudence had the original from their branch of the family. It was only fair."

"Hope, where did you get yours?" I asked. "If you were adopted, how did you find out you were descended from a founder." I'd wondered for a while but didn't know if I could ask, but after these revelations, I didn't think she'd mind.

"That's a long story, but the gist is that I found the medallion in my adoptive parent's effects. At the time, I didn't know what it was, so I showed the girls, and they showed me theirs. With DM on the back of mine, it was obvious the medallion belonged to Daniel Murphy, so we traced his line to the McConnells, which meant either Nadia or some unknown child was my biological parent. Nadia's diary proves she was my mother, and it seemed she'd given the medallion to my parents to keep for me. That heirloom she mentioned." Her voice wobbled a little, and I got up to give her a hug.

I'd never thought about my ancestors or my biological line before. I knew where I came from because Mom constantly reminded me. It must have been hard for Hope not to know.

"Are there more thumb drives floating around that open the

vault?" Simon asked, concern in his voice. "How many? Where are they?"

"There might be a few secure areas in town," Matilda said, nervously biting her lip.

"A few? Mom, please tell me there aren't any more big secrets on the horizon." Devon shook his head. "Just make a list, and we'll go over it in the morning. Right now, I think we've all heard enough for one evening."

CHAPTER THIRTY-NINE

A week after the big reveal, as I'd begun to call it, I still had a hundred or more questions I needed answered, like what happened during the years the McConnells had their medallion and no one could use it in the ritual, but I'd decided I could only absorb so much information in one go. We did find out the original founders' map was also stored in the vault, but there was time for the ladies to explain what the younger generation needed to do before next year's Founders' Day. I wasn't looking forward to performing any kind of ritual, but if it needed to be done... I'd already seen proof of the magic because after the posse had executed the incantation on the outskirts of town while wearing their medallions, there were no more ghostly hauntings.

Friday night was Devon and my pizza and movie night. Pizza at the Blue Sky Café, and a movie of my choice at home, snuggled up with my favorite human and fur baby. As we exited the café, though, Devon seemed to have other ideas. He took my hand and pulled me over to the town gazebo that sat on a large patch of grass in the middle of Luckland.

"Supposed to be a whole slew of shooting stars tonight, Pip. Some sort of meteor shower."

I knew about the meteor shower, though why he wanted to hang out in the gazebo, I had no clue. Suddenly he stopped short, and I followed the direction of his very pointed gaze. The women seemed to have the same idea and had settled themselves in the middle of the gazebo.

"Figures," he muttered.

"We'll go watch from somewhere else. It's fine, Dev. Come on. It's a nice night."

"No, they were all just leaving, weren't you?" He glared at his mother, then shared the same blazing look with the others. "Go. Now."

"I promise you they're all leaving. Now. You, however, are staying. I have something to show you."

Well, that was a Devon I wasn't used to, though it was awfully sexy. Very alpha of him. However, I sensed he had a surprise for me—always a dangerous proposition.

As the women hurriedly scurried off, Devon and I stepped onto the gazebo, and he took out his phone. He tapped the speaker, and the smooth sound of Al Green's *Let's Stay Together* surrounded us as the eaves began to twinkle with little white lights. I gasped, and my stomach did cartwheels.

"You did this for me?"

He smiled softly. "I did."

"It's beautiful."

"*You're* beautiful." He gently pulled me up the stairs onto the platform with a telescope and cushioned benches that allowed a view from any angle.

I took a deep breath and tried to settle my racing pulse. Devon must have done this, though I wasn't sure why. I couldn't help but think he had another surprise in store. Anxiety spiked, but an additional deep breath helped.

"It's truly wonderful, Dev, but the twinkling lights will have to twinkle off, or we won't see any stars."

After a quick tap of his phone, the lights dimmed. He grinned, then strolled over to the scope, and with a few more taps, had it pointed toward the stars.

"Go on, Pip, take a look, and if you see a shooting star, don't forget to make a wish." Though he smiled, something in his voice caught my attention. He seemed nervous. I felt a sudden need to fix that.

"Okay, but first..." I stretched up on my toes, pulled down his face between my palms, and kissed him breathless. Or maybe I was the breathless one. At that moment, I was so far gone in love with that man he could have surprised me with a jack-in-the-box clown, and I'd still kiss him.

I leaned in to look into the scope. I wasn't sure what goddess he'd prayed to, but I'd be damned if there wasn't a shooting star. I smiled and quickly made a wish. When I turned to tell him, I found him on his knees, gazing up at me.

"Did your wish come true?" He looked at me with such adoration, my heart flipped.

I couldn't say a word, so I just nodded furiously as a tear slipped down my face. I'd never imagined how I would feel in a moment like this. I'd kind of just assumed it would never happen, that I was satisfied with the way things were. Apparently, I wasn't. I stared as he held out a small box and opened the lid, revealing an antique, perfect star-cut diamond ring surrounded by small but perfect emeralds. The timeless and elegant ring sparkled under the moonlight. Exactly something Dani knew I would love. Suddenly, her refusal to tell me what she'd done with Simon on the day they'd said they'd gone to the zoo made sense. She must have been scouting rings for Devon.

I glanced back into his eyes and was lost.

"We're meant, Pip, you and I. Always have been. There's never been another for me. There never will be."

He slipped the ring on my finger and stood up, clasping my hands in his. Looking straight into my eyes...my soul... Waiting.

"It's a yes, right?" Hesitation flashed in his eyes, and I briefly remembered Dani demanding how I would like it if she kept asking why Devon hadn't put a ring on it, and I hadn't answered. He'd overheard me that night. Maybe he'd thought I didn't want a ring, and that was why he seemed uncertain now.

"I'm not sure. Did you ask me a question?"

He grinned and gave me a quick kiss. Then another. When he pulled back, his eyes shone. No more hesitation.

"I know we got off to a rocky start..." He smiled mischievously. "You were the firefly always just out of reach." He tucked a stray curl behind my ear, a habit he'd formed. "The one I had to have but could never quite capture. It took me a while to realize capturing you would never do. I just needed you to pause long enough to see me. To choose me."

"I think—no, I know," I said softly, cupping his face. "You've always been mine. My heart has always been yours. It's why I couldn't give it to anyone else."

He tipped his head, and there was something in his expression I'd never seen before. Something sure and steady. Something incredibly wonderful.

"I have a secret," I whispered.

He leaned in. "Tell me."

"Harley."

"Harley James?" Devon smiled. "He's not a secret. I knew about Harley. I, well..." Devon began to pull back. "I might have been the problem."

"No, no, Devon. I mean, I know what you did. I know how you got your scar right here." I gently rubbed a finger along the jagged line above his brow. His badge of honor after beating

Harley James to a pulp for being dishonorable on the night of my high school prom. "I shouldn't have agreed to be his date, but I only said yes to Harley because you didn't ask."

With a sigh, he leaned his forehead against mine. "I'm asking now. Pippa Constance O'Leary, will you say yes? Will you marry me?"

"Yes. Definitely, yes."

He crushed his lips to mine, and I knew with absolute certainty he was totally and forever, my Devon.

Neither of us was surprised when cheers erupted from behind the row of rhododendrons. Nor when a cork popped as the ladies came running, well, jogging, over to the gazebo and up to the platform to join us.

"You can't even give us a moment to celebrate by ourselves?" Devon scowled at Matilda, who grinned like a Cheshire cat.

"You'll have plenty of moments. Kate and I have waited for this since you two were born!"

A flush crept up my face. I looked at Devon, who still had his arms wrapped around me. We shared a glance, and right then, we knew what we had to do, or our lives would be a living hell. Grabbing hands, we held on tight and ran. Straight down Main Street and over to Mystic Manor, then through the front door, which we slammed shut. Then we slid to the floor with our backs to the hardwood door.

Laughing, I didn't think anything could ruin our moment— except the buzz of our phones. As if we could read each other's minds, we threw our phones across the room.

"Now then, where were we?" Devon leaned in and proceeded to give me the most blissfully uninterrupted kiss of our lives.

THE LUCKLAND MYSTERY SERIES

MORE TO COME!

www.scarsdalepublishing.com

www.ingramcontent.com/pod-product-compliance
Lightning Source LLC
Chambersburg PA
CBHW061435210726
48287CB00007B/2223

9 781953 100542